The Temples

of Malplaquet

The Temples of Malplaquet

Andrew Dalton

illustrated by
Jonny Boatfield

The Lutterworth Press

First Published in 2005 by
The Lutterworth Press
P.O. Box 60
Cambridge
CB1 2NT

www.Lutterworth.com
Publishing@Lutterworth.com

ISBN: 0 7188 3046 6 hardback
ISBN: 0 7188 3047 4 paperback

British Library Cataloguing in Publication Data:
A Catalogue Record is available from the British Library

The Temples of Malplaquet takes much of its initial inspiration
(and the quotation on page 178) from *Mistress Masham's Repose*,
one of the less known works of the great English writer, T.H. White

Printed in England by
Athenaeum Press Ltd., Gateshead, Tyne & Wear

To Christopher, Matthew and Lawrence

Contents

MALPLAQUET
a guide to the Temples

N

GRECIAN VALLEY

SCHOOL HOUSE

ELYSIUM

PALLADIA

ACADIA

CASCADIA

① BELL COTTAGE
② PEBBLE ALCOVE.
③ TEMPLE OF FRIENDSHIP.
④ COLD STREAM CUP RUN.
⑤ CASCADE. ⑥ TEMPLE OF BRITISH-
WORTHIES. ⑦ ACACIA TREE ⑧ WOODEN.
JETTY. ⑨ BOAT HOUSE. ⑩ TEMPLE OF-
VENUS. ⑪ GOTHIC TEMPLE ⑫ PALLADIAN.
BRIDGE. ⑬ COLD STREAM.
⑭ QUEEN'S TEMPLE. ⑮ DORIC
ARCH. ⑯ TEMPLE OF ANCIENT
VIRTUE. ⑰ HERMITAGE.
⑱ ROTONDA ⑲ THE JAPS
⑳ GRECIAN TEMPLE

The Way In

Hidden away deep in the English countryside is a huge garden that is full of lakes, bridges, cascades, walks and woods. It also has a most enormous mansion, which is twice as long as Buckingham Palace and three times as attractive. And dotted throughout this garden are dozens of strange buildings.

Very strange buildings.

There's a Gothic Temple, which has *three* sides instead of four, and battlements and a look-out tower like a castle, but huge pointed windows as if it wanted to be a church. Elsewhere, on a small stone pyramid, sits a carved monkey looking into a mirror. There's a bridge with a roof. Statues of Saxon gods and goddesses. Ships' prows sticking out of a tall stone column. A cave of volcanic rock.

They also have the oddest names, such as the Imperial Water-Closet, the Fane of Pastoral Poetry, the Temple of British Worthies, and the Pebble Alcove.

Malplaquet, as perhaps you are already beginning to realise, is not just another old country house and grounds. It's unusual – and special. But what's special is not just what you can see.

It's what you can *feel*.

There's an atmosphere in the gardens. Visitors have always noticed it, but they've never been able to say exactly what it is, or where it comes from.

Until now.

One of them sneezed

1: Across the Water

Malplaquet; an epic garden, created as a type of paradise, one of the great wonders of the eighteenth Century. Containing all manner of buildings by famous architects, its sheer scale must make it Britain's largest work of art. The main mansion is now occupied by Malplaquet School.

County Guide Book

On a warm summer's evening in late July, Mr. Thompson drove the family car through Malplaquet's imposing pair of wrought iron gates, with his wife beside him and their two boys in the back. He slowed down to cast his eyes around the splendid landscape, with its low stretch of water, an old hump-backed bridge, and the road heading up between an avenue of mature trees. Then he uttered the familiar words.

'It's just like another world,' he exclaimed, with deep appreciation, 'or have I said that before?'

'Only every time we come here,' said Charlie, the younger boy, squashed amongst a small mountain of picnic equipment.

'Hurry up, Dad, or we'll miss the fireworks,' urged his brother Jamie, as the car looped gently over the small bridge. Although feeling slightly queasy from too much birthday cake (he was thirteen today), he knew his Dad was right. It was like another world, it really was. The gardens were brilliant; weird buildings and statues hidden amongst trees, secret dens in bushes, and streams, lakes and waterfalls round every corner. It was always fun coming here – and definitely would be this evening.

Mainly because they were going to meet up with Granny – or to be more accurate, the old lady they called 'Granny.' Life was always far more interesting when she was around.

As yet Jamie hadn't been able to work out why.

The Thompsons' car dragged up the long slope and disappeared over the brow of the hill towards the open-air concert and picnic (his parents' idea of a birthday treat). Back down on the bridge, two of the carved stone faces on the decorative urns moved slightly. One on the left, with wild eyes, puffed-out cheeks, and a full beard, gave a wink. Another on the right, normally scowling, gave a huge smile back.

They knew the long sleep was over.

It was the beginning, as described in the ancient Writings.

The Man had arrived.

'Why do we need all this stuff?' groaned Jamie, struggling with his load. 'And where's Base Camp?'

'Very funny,' said Dad, marching on ahead. 'Let's find Granny – it won't be easy in this crowd. My word – that's *really* impressive. Look at that.'

He had rounded the final corner and come to a sudden halt. Jamie caught up, and accidently let slip a chair, two coats, a rug, a large thermos flask, a torch, and a whistle (useful for emergencies such as floods, avalanches, and blizzards). Then he stared. It *was* extraordinary.

The light of the July evening was slowly fading, but on the gently sloping banks of a grassy valley, lined by trees and bushes, were hundreds of pin-pricks of light, as if all the stars above had floated down to earth and were hovering around in this vast hollow. These flickering candles were wedged into bottles, or fixed inside small metal lanterns hanging from poles. Groups of picnickers were sat around, chatting and laughing quietly, enjoying their food and each other's company.

Dominating one end of the valley was the pale-cream mass of a huge Greek temple, like the Acropolis above Athens, columns on all sides, with stone figures crowning the high points of the roof. In its front portico sat a small chamber orchestra, the men in dinner jackets, and the ladies in dark dresses, gently playing some Music for a Summer's Evening. Coloured spotlights of blue and green were skimming around, catching the branches of nearby cedar trees that were silhouetted against the oranges and pinks of the sunset.

Even as the Thompson family watched, quite spellbound, the whole galaxy of lights began to sharpen and to twinkle more strongly. There was an air of quiet mystery, of suspense. It almost looked 'Magical,' said Mr. Thompson, 'absolutely *magical*. And . . . yes . . . I do believe that could well be her. . . . '

He was squinting towards the temple. Just below it, in prime position, lay a picnic rug that was barricaded by large bags, an electric buggy and a folding chair. Standing in the centre was an old lady, waving a rolled-up umbrella in time to the music, but now and again pointing it threateningly towards any intruders.

'Yep, 'fraid so, that's her,' replied Jamie cheerfully, feeling very proud. Granny spotted them, and conducted even more wildly with both arms. The Thompsons wandered over, and Jamie received a big hug. People nearby were relieved that some guests had turned up to protect them.

'Well, how is the birthday boy?' she said enthusiastically, handing over a large card in a bright red envelope. 'Feeling any older? Do you know, some people think boys come of age at thirteen – so perhaps I should call you a birthday *man*.'

Granny lived down by the Octagon Lake in a small cottage. Rather wonderfully, it was built onto the back of a classical temple by the Bell Gate entrance to the gardens. For years, whenever the Thompsons had walked down that path, she'd always been there, leaning over the fence, and keen to chat. Before long, she was their own particular granny; the two boys had no grandparents of their own, she herself had no living relatives, and so it had suited both sides to adopt each other. She quickly became a very convenient and interesting baby-sitter; she had an inexhaustible supply of fascinating stories about Malplaquet when it was a country-house, played a mean game of cards, and could even score well on Jamie's favourite computer game of 'Myths and Legends.'

'I haven't got your present here, I'm afraid,' she apologised. '*Much* too big to carry. You'll have to come for it tomorrow morning.'

Sounds promising, thought Jamie. 'What time?'

'As soon as you want, my dear. I'm always up with the birds.' Fitting a small jacket, no longer than three inches, onto a doll, she placed it in her sewing-bag. She spent hours and hours making such tiny clothes, often selling her exquisite handiwork on the WI stall at the local market. Her skills with a needle and thread were legendary.

Inexplicable things shouldn't happen when you're merely playing 'Hide and Seek' with a whinging brother.

'It's not fair, you hiding first,' protested Charlie, 'you've been here loads more times than me. You know all the best places.'

'I won't go far, honest, and I'll come out in five minutes if you can't find me,' said Jamie, desperate to get going. 'Shut your eyes and start counting.' He darted off.

On a previous visit Jamie had spotted a few badger sets bursting up under some bushes. The perfect spot, he realised; with the foliage and small mounds of earth to hide behind, Charlie would never find him. He ran over, dropped to his knees, and pushed aside a few branches. As he began to wriggle in, his face barely above the ground, he pressed his right hand on a scattering of fresh earth at the sloping entrance to a hole. He looked down and then didn't move his hand any further.

Next to it was a line of tiny prints. Shoeprints. Leading into the tunnel.

Jamie stared at them, stunned. He didn't know what to think.

'I can see your feet!' shouted a familiar voice from behind. 'Got you!'

Jamie groaned, squirmed back out on his elbows and stood up, brushing the dirt off his trousers. 'Okay . . . look, let's pack this in and do something else.'

'You *always* do that when it's my turn!'

'Don't be stupid, you know I don't! Just grow up.' Jamie (for once) wasn't in a mood for an argument with his younger brother.

'I'm telling. Just because it's your birthday. . . .' Charlie ran off to complain to their parents.

Jamie's mind was buzzing about the footprints in the soil. There had to be an obvious explanation for them – like, for example, some kids playing with a toy figure. But right inside some bushes? He slowly sat down on the grassy slope opposite the temple to try to think about it.

The final streaks of the sunset were beginning to fade, the darkening hollow was peppered by flickering lights, and the musicians were playing something gentle and relaxing. Then he heard it.

Or rather, heard *them*.

Two voices, both very faint. Like picking up a distant channel on his radio.

Startled, Jamie glanced around. Nobody was near him, and yet he could definitely hear a conversation. He screwed up his eyes to concentrate.

There was the odd word or two – 'crowds' and 'fireworks.' Then a longer snatch of conversation.

'. . . the new Assistant Guide.'

'Nigriff will know.'

Then silence. What on earth was going on? Was he hearing things? And who was 'Nigriff'? He listened again, but there was only classical music, easy and relaxed chatter, the chink of glasses and the distinctive sound of Charlie moaning.

In a slight daze, Jamie got to his feet and shuffled slowly back to his family.

Mr. Thompson spotted him first and noticed his look of deep thought – which struck his Father as unusual. 'Hello, Jamie. Are you alright?'

'I'm, er, fine,' offered Jamie, not that confidently.

'Isn't it Charlie's turn to hide?' added his Mother. Charlie smugly folded his arms in satisfaction and stared at him.

Jamie shook his head. 'It's too dark for Hide and Seek. You can't see properly.'

Granny nodded, her eyes fixed calmly and steadily on Jamie. He reckoned she knew something.

At that moment the musicians completed their performance, and a man in a crumpled cream suit walked over to the microphone at the top of the steps. He tapped it, making a loud clonking noise, and announced, in an embarrassed manner, 'Ladies and Gentlemen, I'm afraid that the final movement of Schubert's Unfinished Symphony ended sooner than we had anticipated, so there will now be a short delay while the Pyrotechnic Ignition Operatives take up their positions.'

'Sounds like fireworks,' said Granny, 'time to light the blue touchpaper and retire. I'm off. Busy day tomorrow.'

She gathered up her bits and pieces, packing them into the luggage compartment on her electric buggy. Jamie called the vehicle her 'GT' – short for 'Golf Trolley.' Downhill with a following wind it could overtake most pedestrians.

She turned to Jamie. 'You *must* come and see me in the morning.'

He nodded – and immediately, much to his astonishment, heard a bell frantically being rung. Not a church bell, but something much smaller, like the one teachers ring in a playground. It was clear and ringing out across the gardens, but nobody seemed to be reacting at all. But he did spot that Granny was watching him.

She drew closer, and whispered in his ear. 'You can hear the bell, can't you? It's time you knew. Tomorrow. Don't tell anyone.' She smiled, revved the engine, scattered startled picnickers, and then ambled away at top speed, headlights lighting up the bushes on either side of the path.

The first fireworks exploded above the crowds in a blaze of coloured lights, stars bursting into huge parachutes and showers of sparkling rain. They were impressive, but far bigger fireworks were going off in Jamie's head.

Who had made those footprints? What *were* those voices he'd heard? Why was he the only one that heard the bell? What did she mean about it being time he knew? It wasn't just a present he wanted from Granny.

He wanted some answers.

At her cottage, Granny was packing away her sewing stuff and placing three dolls in their shoe-boxes. She was muttering to herself. 'Well, so far, so good. I think at long last we have a winner.' One doll seemed to be getting particular care, having its green and white check quilt gently tucked down each side. It was an older male doll, a white shirt collar just visible under the bedclothes, its eyes closed on its expressionless face. 'Tomorrow,' she said, 'we should find out the truth.' The doll didn't reply of course. It was way past its bedtime.

Next morning Jamie awoke before his alarm. Slipping out of bed, and checking there was no sign of Charlie, he sat down at his desk, and stared at the screen of his brand-new laptop. The pipes on his screensaver were tying themselves up in knots, much like his brain was doing. His mind was full of the strange things that had happened the previous night – tiny footprints, disembodied voices, distant bells. A memorable birthday really. He knocked the mouse into life, and then entered his password (four asterisks – nobody would ever guess that).

Opening a file, he headed it *Nothing Special*. Another brilliant security device.

He then opened up a second called *Not Worth Looking In*, which led to *Seriously Boring Stuff*. Nobody would ever make the effort to go this far, not even Charlie, who had dedicated his life to uncovering Jamie's secrets. He began to type.

> *Sunday July 23ʳᵈ. Weird at the fireworks last night; heard and saw some odd things, like voices without people, and bells. Granny said it was time, and I shouldn't tell anybody. Maybe I'm going to find out I'm adopted, I'm old enough to be told now. Charlie can't be adopted, he's got the Thompson nose.*

Over breakfast, Jamie tested his theory. Mr. Thompson, sipping on a strong coffee, was surprised to be asked, 'Dad, exactly what *do* I get from you?'

Deciding it wasn't a subtle request for more pocket-money,

he had a stab at answering it in a sensible way. Well, sensible for 8.15 on a Sunday morning. 'Let me see. Apart from extraordinary good looks and an amazing physique, I'd probably say an unfair share of my hard-earned money and the best years of my life. Is that enough, or do you think you've got a raw deal?'

Jamie realised his Dad wasn't awake yet, so he decided to beat a hasty retreat and get on his bike to check out Granny's big birthday present.

Minutes later, raising clouds of dust on the track that led to her cottage, he sent a group of rabbits scurrying for cover – apart from a single white one that ran on ahead and then stopped. It looked at him sideways. Jamie pulled hard on his brakes and burst out laughing.

'So, Mr. Rabbit, do you know what's going on?'

'Doubt if he knows, Jamie . . . but you could ask the squirrels.' The answer came from behind him; a girl's voice. Just his luck; great time to be talking to a rabbit.

Turning round, and feeling embarrassed, he saw Vicky standing in the farmyard entrance. They had known each other for years. Three years older than Jamie, she often came up this way for riding lessons. She also worked in the gardens as a Volunteer some weekends.

'Oh, hi, Vicky. Um, it's just, er, a game. See you soon. Bye.'

He sped off, determined not to chat to any more animals. After thirty seconds of thumping over potholes, and a final screech of brakes, he was at the cottage on the outer edge of Malplaquet gardens. Granny was in the yard, giving her plants a good water with the hosepipe.

'Morning, Jamie, up bright and early?' she said breezily, happily spraying her windows and the back porch as she turned. 'I wonder why. . . .'

Jamie grinned. She turned off the tap, noticing with surprise that her windows were sopping wet.

'Come on, it's in the shed. Follow me.' He watched as she pretended to have some difficulty turning the key. The door creaked open, and as his eyes got used to the light, he saw a rowing boat, a little longer than him, leaning against the far wall.

'There,' said the pleased old lady, 'what do you think? Amazing the kits you can get these days. The latest open-topped model, two-seater, built for looks *and* performance. Bit sluggish going uphill though.'

Jamie was seriously impressed. He inspected the pair of smooth oars, ran his hands along the varnished wood, and imagined himself pulling hard across the Octagon and the Eleven-Acre Lake.

'Excellent! Thanks a lot – can I try it out now?'

'I knew you'd ask. How about later? When the sun's been on the water,' replied Granny to Jamie's dismay. 'Come inside for a Birthday Brownie instead – I bet you bolted your breakfast down.'

Once inside, while she sorted out the refreshments, he allowed his eyes to drift round the sitting-room.

It was all very familiar. Lots of books, piles of newspapers, bags full of knitting and sewing, and plenty of her 'knick-knacks' on windowsills. On the upright piano was a collection of photos, including one of the Thompson family at Christmas, and one of Granny when she was a little girl (bright-eyed, glasses, hair in pigtails). Elsewhere were small white pottery ornaments with crests, a pile of letters, a vase of flowers – and a very special item in a glass case.

Inside, neatly folded, lay some beautiful and intricate lace fabric; to be precise, it was part of her wedding-dress (the top of the veil, he'd been told). Jamie was no expert in such matters, but he knew the workmanship of this piece was superb.

He wandered over to the semi-circular polished table by the window. On it lay three dolls that Granny was making clothes for. The sunlight was pouring in, showing up some dust on them. Jamie spotted a brightly-coloured feather duster, and, deciding to help her out, gave their faces a quick brush.

This was the moment that Jamie would never forget.

One of them sneezed.

Jamie dropped the duster and shot back into the chair. The tiny person sat up, hurriedly pulled out a minuscule handkerchief, blew his nose loudly and ostentatiously, and said, 'Goodness me, how extraordinary!'

Jamie didn't have a chance to reply (and frankly it was difficult anyway, with his mouth stuck wide open), because just at that point Granny walked in with a tray of drinks.

'Now we can sit down properly and . . . oh, I see you've already met,' she said quite calmly. 'Good. That helps a lot.' She put the tray down, sat beside Jamie, and smiled at him. 'Let me introduce you to one of my very best friends.'

2: Passing the Tests

'Jamie, this fine gentleman standing in front of you is Nigriff, Senior Imperial Archivist. During his most celebrated career, he has also been appointed Chief Historian (2nd Papyrus Division), and Most Notable Librarian (First Editions). And by the way,' she whispered, leaning forwards, 'your mouth is wide open. To a person only six inches high, that's a very frightening sight.'

Jamie closed his mouth slowly and deliberately, not taking his eyes off the little figure, who was still dusting himself down and sniffing. So this was Nigriff. He had a mop of wavy brown hair that was greying at the edges, and he was wearing a white shirt (open-necked), a dark jacket, and a pair of trousers that were tucked into his long socks – which were bright yellow (the fashion amongst Archivists that year).

Granny whispered, 'He's waiting for you to say something.'

Jamie had never spoken to a person that small. He simply stammered, 'Ar . . . Ar . . . Archivist?'

Nigriff raised an eyebrow in surprise. Granny stepped in. 'I'm sure you've heard of them, Jamie – they look after archives, places where they store old documents. Nigriff is in charge of a remarkable collection; some of the writings date back nearly three hundred years.'

Jamie was impressed. He was obviously in the presence of someone of real stature and importance, even if he didn't know

exactly *what* this figure was. It was time to be polite. He took a
deep breath, looked steadily at the Senior Imperial Archivist,
and said, as respectfully as he could, 'Good morning, Mr. Nigriff.
I'm, er, pleased to meet you.'

'Young sir,' came the confident reply, 'I am most honoured to
make your acquaintance too, and I trust you will forgive me for
my rude bout of sneezing.'

Jamie nodded. His next comment was understandable in the
circumstances.

'Are you a Borrower?'

'A *borrower*?' Nigriff retorted, very indignant. 'Indeed *not*, sir!'
He was struggling to find the right words and stay calm. 'Is that my
reputation? A borrower? An eminent Librarian, branded in such a
manner! An *Elysian*, with a distinguished pedigree, to be. . . .'

Granny leapt to Jamie's defence against this barrage.

'Nigriff, they're characters in a children's story,' she
explained gently. 'They're about your size, and they borrow things
to survive in the human world.'

Nigriff seemed slightly pacified. 'Madam, I am pleased to
hear that they exist only in the human imagination, but I fail to
comprehend why they are so respected if they, as you appear to
suggest, live completely by borrowing.'

'Good point, Nigriff, spoken like a true Librarian,' replied
Granny. 'Anyway, Jamie, I hope you realise that there are plenty
of others like Nigriff. Well, nobody *exactly* like him of course,
but there is a huge population out there.'

'*Huge*?' queried Jamie, thinking it was an odd word to choose.

'Well, no, I mean there are hundreds of them.'

'I nearly saw one last night,' admitted Jamie. Granny sipped
her drink. 'I thought as much,' she murmured.

'There were some shoeprints by a badger's hole. Is that where
they live?'

'Some do.'

'So what are they, I mean, are *you*, Mr. Nigriff?'

Granny and Nigriff exchanged a long look. She put her cup
back on its saucer, and padded over to her bookcase. She lifted
a well-thumbed volume off the top shelf.

'Jamie, you've obviously read *The Borrowers*. You must have come across this one as well; it's very famous. *Gulliver's Travels.*' She handed it over.

Jamie stared at the book. The book about a man shipwrecked on an island. An island full of little people. Little people probably much like the one in front of him.

'Nigriff said he was an Elysian,' said Granny quietly, 'but it's not as simple as that. You see, a long time ago, Nigriff's ancestors lived on the island of Lilliput.'

Jamie looked slowly up at her, then at Nigriff (who was standing with his arms folded, looking important), and then back to the book. 'So this children's story. . . .'

'. . . really happened,' finished Granny. 'But very few humans know that.'

Jamie idly turned over the first few pages, and spotted the map of the island. 'So where is Lilliput?'

'I'm afraid it's long gone. Malplaquet's the only place where they live now.'

'Did Gulliver bring them here?'

'No, not him,' Granny replied. 'He only took some animals. Let me show you the end of the story.' She turned to a page at the back. 'Here it is. *I took with me six Cows and two Bulls alive, with as many Ewes and Rams, intending to carry them into my own Country and propagate the Breed. . . . I would gladly have taken a Dozen of the Natives. . . .*'

'Suffice to say there was a later incident, young Sir,' said Nigriff rapidly, cutting in, 'but there are few historical records on this matter. It all happened long ago, in what you call the early eighteenth century.'

Jamie thought for a moment. 'Three hundred years ago? You lot have been here that long – and no-one's ever found you? Mind you, you are hard to spot.'

Granny continued. 'You must also remember, Jamie, that when this place was a country-house, before it became a school, the gardens were virtually empty. Just the estate-workers, and the odd Duke or Duchess, not lots of National Trust visitors. The Lilliputians also had a perfect hiding-place; a small island in the Eleven-Acre Lake, overgrown with brambles. Nobody ever went there.'

'An island on the Eleven-Acre?' said Jamie, looking puzzled. 'There isn't one. Has that gone as well?' This was sounding more and more weird – small people appearing, two big islands *dis*appearing. . . .

Nigriff, sat cross-legged and tackling a large crumb of cake, gave Jamie a hard stare. 'Sir, the island was removed . . .' and then suddenly, without warning, he went completely stiff, absolutely motionless, one hand full of Brownie half-way to his mouth.

Before Granny or Jamie could react, they were startled by a cheery greeting near the door. 'Hiya! I knew you'd be here. What did you get?'

The newcomer was Charlie, very excited, dropping his bike on the ground. Jamie was annoyed by the interruption, but Granny was as welcoming as ever.

'Charlie, how lovely to see you! What a nice surprise.'

'Is that his present? Some dolls?'

Jamie scowled. 'Very funny,' he muttered. 'Does Mum know you're here?'

Granny intervened quickly. 'Now, now,' she said. 'Have a look out in the shed, Charlie. I'll just put a few things away here.' She picked up the three dolls, including the one with a half-eaten cake stuck in its hand.

'Okay,' breezed Charlie, giving Jamie a self-satisfied grin. The two of them watched him go back out to the yard.

'A bit of a close call,' breathed Granny, 'but I think we're alright. Nigriff must have seen him coming down the track.' They wandered into the kitchen.

'Brothers are a pain,' grumbled Jamie. 'Lucky that Nigriff noticed.'

Nigriff relaxed and spoke up. 'It may surprise you, Sir, but my reflexes are remarkably efficient. I can do nothing extremely quickly.'

'To be honest, Jamie, I think we'd have been okay anyway,' added Granny, keeping her voice down. 'It's an odd thing, and Nigriff and I have never really understood it, but most humans can't see the Lilliputians – and those that can usually have no idea they're alive. All Charlie saw were three dolls on the table.'

'So how come *I* know that Nigriff's alive?' asked Jamie, puzzled but also pleased at being so talented.

'As I said, I'm not sure, but you do have a special *feeling* for things round here; I noticed it years ago. Anyway, I've got to show you something in the grounds. Nigriff will be safe in here while we're gone.' She bent down, placed the Archivist inside one of the cupboards, and locked the door. 'He'll be okay. If the worst happens, there's an escape hole at the back. Let's go and see Charlie.'

He was already back from the shed and tucking into two of the cakes, one in each hand. 'Smart boat! Can we try it out?'

'Not today, Charlie. The final coat of varnish has to dry really hard, and I'm showing Jamie a couple of the temples – for his school holiday project.'

'Okay, count me out. I hate history,' said Charlie. He picked up *Gulliver's Travels*. 'I'll stay here and look at this.'

'Fine,' said Granny, 'it's a good story. Come on Jamie, plenty to tell you.' Charlie smirked at his brother, glad to be missing the history lesson.

Outside, the two of them entered the tall wooden gates in the stone boundary wall. Immediately in front lay the Octagon Lake, beautifully silent at this time of the morning, and beyond it rose a vast diagonally-striped lawn, presided over by the magnificent South Front of Malplaquet House itself. They turned right and scrunched along the gravel boundary path. There was no-one else about.

'What about Dad? Has he seen Nigriff or any of the others?' asked Jamie, still thinking about the Lilliputians being invisible to most people. 'He knows *everything* about Malplaquet.'

Granny shook her head. 'I don't think he's ever got beyond the facts in the guidebooks. You're different – you've virtually lived in these grounds. Always on your bike, kicking footballs, fishing with a net, messing about near the water. You do *know* something about Malplaquet – but you also seem to *feel* it.'

They had come to a stop in front of the Temple of Friendship, the only ruined monument in the grounds. Its rough walls were open to the sky, and gaping doorways and arches framed views over the gardens and outlying fields. The old lady and her young companion sat down on a wooden bench by the front wall, looking down towards the lake and the Palladian Bridge.

And then it happened. Leaning back against the temple, Jamie suddenly felt his shoulders becoming warm, in fact extremely hot. There was a smell of smoke, and then a roar behind him as the flames quickly took hold, and he heard the crackle of blazing timbers. The Temple had caught fire! He leapt forward off the seat, turning round to stare at the inferno.

But it wasn't burning – in fact it wasn't doing anything. It was the same as ever; a rough but solid ruin, bathed in the morning sunlight. Totally confused, Jamie gingerly touched the front wall. It was cold and damp. There was no sign of a fire anywhere, and he felt a complete fool.

Granny, however, ignored his antics, acting as if nothing had happened. She simply got to her feet. 'That's better, time to move on.'

'B . . . b . . . but . . . the wall,' Jamie stammered, not wanting to say anything but very bewildered, 'it was *red hot* just now!'

'Ah, yes . . . the heat. One of the odd things about Friendship,' she said nonchalantly. 'It's the morning sun, warms it up.'

'But it was on fire! And I could smell smoke!'

'Smell? Are you sure?' She was suddenly interested. 'Well, I don't know, honestly I don't . . . we ought to get back and see Nigriff.' She bustled off in a hurry.

Their route took them alongside the lake, past another temple. The Pebble Alcove was like a stone shelter, about five metres high, with a curved inner face. This was covered with an amazing collection of different coloured stones, pressed into the cement in a variety of animal shapes or patterns. In the centre was a large coat of arms with the Latin phrase, *Templa Quam Dilecta*.

' "How Beautiful are thy Temples" – a good motto, and they are particularly beautiful when you need to rest old legs,' groaned Granny, breathing hard after her short burst of energy, and settling herself down on the inner bench. 'I do like these patterns, especially that butterfly there. Which is *your* favourite, Jamie?'

He wasn't into making polite conversation, but just to please her, he had a quick look on either side behind him, and then pointed up to his right, at the outline of a mermaid.

As he did so, a rippling curtain of mist dropped silently down across the entrance to the Alcove. On it appeared moving images; a sea-shore, waves lapping on the beach, crowds of people. He sniffed the air, full of salt and seaweed. He heard excited shouts, and words that sounded foreign. Then the picture faded as quickly as it had appeared, and there was Granny's soft reassuring voice. 'Yes, the mermaid . . . the sea-people appear . . . ,' before adding more loudly, 'Right, that's plenty for one morning.' She got up and set off along the path through the trees. Jamie quickly followed, tagging along at her side, quiet and thoughtful, but funnily enough not frightened.

Near the cottage Granny suddenly spoke up. 'You're *definitely* the right person for the job.'

Jamie stopped and looked up at her. 'Job? What job?'

'Oh, nothing difficult, just helping me to protect the little people. I'm not getting any younger, and they're definitely becoming livelier. Far too much energy. You could start this afternoon; my new Assistant Guide.'

Jamie's heart missed a beat; 'Assistant Guide' – the phrase the voices at the picnic had mentioned. He had to agree. 'Okay, I don't mind helping. Could be fun.'

'Good. I need to chat to your Mum and Dad. Pop back home with Charlie, and I'll phone to see if you can come and stay with me. How does a week sound?' Jamie nodded. 'Mind,' she continued furtively, 'not a *word* to anyone about the job, especially Charlie.'

Not difficult, thought Jamie, he'll be the last person I'll tell.

At the cottage, Granny told Charlie that he could have a go in the new boat soon, and that Jamie might be staying 'to help with some little things to do with the temples'. Charlie wasn't bothered; it sounded more like schoolwork. Jamie sneaked into the kitchen with her to say cheerio to Nigriff.

As she lifted up the little figure (clutching a corner of a biscuit), Jamie whispered in her ear, 'There's a couple of other things, Granny.'

'What's that?'

'Well, at least I know that Dad is my Dad, even if I haven't got his nose, and I won't talk to any rabbits on the way back, especially the white ones.'

Before either she or Nigriff could say anything, he had run out of the cottage and the two brothers were racing on their bikes back up the track.

Nigriff was scratching his chin and looking anxious.

'Madam, we have known each other for many moons, and of course I do respect your judgement, but can it be that Master Jamie is indeed, *"Our Fount of Wisdom, the True Source of all Pure Knowledge and Insight"*?' Granny smiled and nodded. Nigriff frowned and carried on. 'Judging by his final comments, he has the oddest relationships with humans and animals. I must ask you again; are you totally confident of this boy?'

'Nigriff, he's *not* a boy. Remember what it says? *A Child no more? The Man appears?* There is absolutely no doubt he's the one. I told you last night about the bell, and the two Tests today proved the point.'

Nigriff leaned forward. 'So I assume he had *Warmth in Friendship*?'

'Warmth?' queried Granny. 'We nearly had roast teenager! He leapt off the bench as if he'd been scorched. And he said he *smelt* the fire as well – extraordinary.'

Nigriff became serious. 'Not necessarily extraordinary, Madam.' He spoke deliberately. 'Presumably, from what you're saying, he matched the third sign, the sea-people?'

Granny nodded. 'He chose the mermaid straightaway, although he seemed to go into a bit of a trance, sniffing the air and everything – as if he was actually at the seaside.'

'Hmm,' mused Nigriff. 'These are extremely strong responses.'

'Maybe, Nigriff, but the crucial point is that he's agreed to be the Assistant Guide. It's what we've been waiting for – the new Empire can begin!'

Nigriff nodded slowly. 'You are of course right, Madam – it is indeed momentous. But I'm concerned. . . .' He hesitated, picking his words. 'The young man did feel warm, and he selected the correct picture . . . but his *other* senses were deeply affected. We must consider *all* the prophecies, as I have often . . . '

'Nigriff, for goodness' sake, that's not an issue at the moment!' interrupted Granny, a sudden sharpness in her voice. 'Look, I know you've read far more about this place than I have, and lots of questions are bothering you, but let's stick to what we can be sure about.' Nigriff looked suitably squashed and waited for her to finish. 'We know what the old prophecy says, and Jamie has successfully passed all its Three Tests. Of course he still has to prove his actual ability, but so far so good.'

'Indeed Madam, but all I can say is that I am mindful of *all* the prophecies – and past enemies.'

'That's exactly the point, Nigriff – *past* enemies. So let's stop moping around, I need to make a phone-call. Jamie should be home by now, unless he's been chatting to a rabbit or two. . . .'

The timing of the brothers was perfect for lunch, which was one of Mum's famous Sunday roasts. Charlie was out of breath and sweating (he came second in the bike-race) and Jamie was dead pleased with himself. Mum spotted his good mood.

'Hello, you've obviously had a fine morning. Fresh air and exercise – or just the birthday present? Have you used it yet?'

'Not yet, but it's brilliant,' panted Jamie, 'and Granny's going to call soon.'

On cue, the phone rang. Dad walked into the hall to answer it. 'Hello, yes, the present's a real hit, thanks ever so much.' He was speaking loudly for Granny's benefit, which meant Jamie could hear the conversation (or at least one side of it).

'No, that's fine, I can't see that being a problem. . . . Yes, I'm pleased that he's so interested in the garden buildings, he might be an architect yet. . . . No, archi*tect*, not archi*vist* . . . , yes, I know there's nothing wrong with being an archivist . . . but it's a bit like being a librarian, isn't it. . . . yes, some of my best friends are as well. . . no, it's not an easy job . . . okay, see you soon, bye.'

He sat down, a frustrated look on his face. 'Her hearing's definitely getting worse. Went on and on about archivists and librarians. Will you be safe with her for a whole week, Jamie?' His eldest son nodded and grinned, his mouth full of roast potato.

After lunch was packing.

Mum gathered a mound of sensible clothing for all sorts of appalling climactic conditions, ranging from severe frosts to sudden typhoons (apparently a common risk in deepest Buckinghamshire in late July).

Dad handed over a couple of guidebooks about Malplaquet, and a pair of binoculars – 'for looking at small details.'

Charlie dropped unsubtle hints about using his brother's computer and CD player.

Jamie scoured his bedroom and found useful things such as his camera, writing pad, mini-toolkit, and loads of stuff that would be extremely interesting if you were only fifteen centimetres high. Finally he checked his Charlie-proof password on his computer, and changed it to 'Charlieisgreat.' He'd never expect that one.

That evening Jamie sat back in Granny's chair in astonishment. 'Scrabble? You can't be serious, Nigriff?'

'It will help you learn some of our words, sir – most useful in your new role.'

As the game developed, Jamie noticed for the first time just how exhausting – even dangerous – Scrabble could be. Nigriff insisted on moving his tiles himself – dragging them out of the bag, sliding them across to his wooden rack, and, when it was his turn, carrying them (three at a time) onto the board. This required stepping over earlier words, so Jamie offered to help, wanting to avoid the rare sight of a Scrabble player being stretchered off the pitch. Nigriff, however, was determined to face the tough physical challenges of the game.

'Thank you, Master Jamie, I appreciate your kindness, but during my working life I have carried some weighty documents, and I am still capable of delivering a few letters.'

Nevertheless, the little man did have some advantages. Jamie realised that when Nigriff crawled inside the bag to collect the tiles, the Archivist's eyes might not be fully shut – and he was also the main authority on *one* language in this bi-lingual game.

'SWONAD? What's that, Nigriff?' asked Jamie (on the third round).

'An actor, sir, particularly one with a fine singing voice.'

(Sixth turn) 'CLAWVANE? Another actor?'

'No, of course not, sir. A clawvane is the seed that some trees drop; they twirl in a gyrating fashion, like your helicopters. There are lots of clawvanes in these gardens – I'm surprised you haven't seen them.'

Later the little historian added LIMBLEK to their vocabulary (38 points – a gambling term for three consecutive wins at the rat races), closely followed by VAZEDIR (42 points), obviously the largest and nastiest fish in the Malplaquet lakes, and finally Nigriff's greatest triumph came with DREYSNOL (92 points, including an extra 50 for using all of his letters). Jamie and Granny were prepared by now to accept any definition, no matter how outrageous.

'Don't tell me, Nigriff, it's a medical term for someone, frequently a child under six, with a very heavy cold, especially in January?' asked Jamie sarcastically.

'No, sir, that's DRISNIL. Easily confused. No, a dreysnol is a bag for carrying food in.'

When the final scores were added up, there were no surprises.

'Well done, Nigriff. You've won yet again. And first prize is showing our young visitor around all of the four provinces of Malplaquet tomorrow.' Granny looked straight at him. '*All* of them, Nigriff. Do you understand what I'm saying?'

'Of course, Madam. Trust me; I will show him as much as I possibly can. A guided tour of the highlights of Malplaquet. Everything that is worth seeing.'

'Hmm,' muttered Granny, not sounding at all convinced.

Jamie was delighted and found it hard to get to sleep that night. 'The four provinces . . . everything that is worth seeing.' What would he be shown tomorrow? Lots more little people?

3: A Voyage of Discovery

'Let's hope we don't capsize, Nigriff,' said Jamie ominously. It was early morning, and the two of them were just setting off across the Octagon Lake in the new rowing-boat. 'I'd hate a vazedir to get you.'

'A what, sir?'

'You know, those very large fish. We were talking about them last night. Vazedirs. Really nasty apparently.'

'Oh yes, those. I *do* apologise, sir, I didn't hear you correctly, yes, indeed, the dreaded vazedirs . . . *very* vicious creatures.' Jamie dipped the oars in the water, and headed with a grin on his face towards the middle of the lake. This was really good fun – and his tour-guide being cocooned in a large lifejacket of bubble-wrap made it even more enjoyable. For whenever Nigriff accidently squashed the plastic sheet, it emitted a small explosion, which surprised and embarrassed him. He was trying to explain to Jamie about the provinces.

'The esteemed Granny, sir, insists that I tell you about *each* of the four. Naturally I will do my best, but I may perchance spend more time on some than on others.'

'Sure, Nigriff. Which province are we in now?' Jamie asked, pulling steadily on the oars, pleased with his smooth style so far. Olympics here we come.

'None, sir. This Octagon Lake is *common* water, so you might meet all four types of Lilliputians here. Other parts of Malplaquet are also common land, but they're not the most attractive areas.' Loud pop. 'Do forgive me, sir.'

'I suppose you go round the other provinces a lot?' asked Jamie, looking around him.

Nigriff was shocked. 'I beg your pardon? For what reason?'

'Well, I don't know – maybe to meet other people, to see what they're like.'

'But we *know* what they're like – and that's why we don't need to meet them. On occasion we may *have* to pass through another province, but one doesn't take any longer than is strictly necessary.'

Jamie was surprised by Nigriff's attitude; he'd assumed that they all got on well with each other. 'But you all speak the same language, don't you?' he asked.

'Most of the original Lilliputian language has disappeared in favour of English, young sir, although some older people do retain our ancestral habits and thus speak in capital letters. Nevertheless, each province has a few local words. For example, the terrifying vazedir is known as a 'lenal' in Cascadia, the province we can now see through that old archway above their main cascade. Do apply the brakes.'

Jamie stopped rowing, and looked across at an opening in a stone wall, framing a view of the Eleven-Acre Lake stretching out below it.

'Right, Cascadia,' sighed Nigriff, sounding bored. '93.4% water, air similar, climate damp, inhabitants called Cascadians. Noted for sporting and athletic ability, they do well at the Inter-Provincial Games but little else. Dragon-Fly surfing a speciality.'

'Sounds impressive,' said Jamie approvingly.

'If you say so, sir,' replied Nigriff, not at all impressed. He quickly continued. 'Their most notable building is the Temple of Venus, with its own underground swimming-pool – a rather frivolous touch.' He stopped. 'That's all you require. Now, if you turn round, to the east you will be facing the frontier of Palladia.'

Jamie couldn't believe that Nigriff was already on the second province. 'Have we finished with Cascadia?'

'Indeed, sir. I must leave enough time for other . . . weightier matters,' the Archivist replied, a touch of irritation in his voice. He swivelled round on the seat, emitted a rude noise, and looked in the opposite direction. Jamie began to row again. The boat was gently rocking and splashing, but he could still hear lots of birdsong from across the water. 'Sounds like plenty of wildlife over there, Nigriff.'

'Correct, sir, I am delighted you have realised; 'wild' is *exactly* the right word. It is incredibly uncivilised.'

'No, I mean birds, all the chirping – listen.'

Nigriff did so, and then smiled to himself. 'Master Jamie, I'm afraid those noises are the Palladians themselves. For some bizarre reason they have perfected the ability to communicate via whistles as well as words. Why they have degraded the beautiful rhythms of spoken language with fowl twitterings escapes me.'

'Sounds like they're good at it,' replied Jamie, who had always wanted to whistle really well. 'But don't they get confused with the birds? You know, mistaking the mating-call of a thrush for being told supper's ready?'

'I am sure that's extremely likely, sir. Although I am told that they are on good terms with the creatures; apparently they have constructed many dwellings in the trees. They are capable builders; some of their homes are hidden in the cliff-face of the garden wall.'

'And is all of this area Palladia?' asked Jamie, shielding his eyes from the glare on the lake.

'Yes, sir, apart from the Japanese Gardens beyond the Palladian Bridge. But about those, you will need to ask the good lady herself.'

'Why? Can't you tell me?'

'You will need to ask the good lady herself,' he repeated, his voice firm.

Interesting, thought Jamie. Nigriff – keeping quiet? He's hiding something.

The expedition's leader found his voice again. 'And now –
let us set sail for the fair province of Elysium. To the oars –
pull! The wind is filling our sails!'

Two minutes later they were moving carefully up a small reedy
inlet. En route, Nigriff had been singing a lengthy saga about a
great hero from the past, Rentur the Wise. This mighty leader
had conquered distant lands such as the Plains of Nurobob,
discovered a totally new chemical element, and composed
anthems for choirs of over two hundred people. Funnily enough,
in the last line it mentioned he was an Elysian.

Once sung-out, Nigriff climbed up onto the prow of the ship,
spread out his arms and in his loudest voice shouted, 'Hail to
thee, fairest province, hail to thee Elysium! Land of Wisdom, the
Home of Heroes, the Source of Beauty and Virtue! The intrepid
travellers bid you welcome!'

Two early-morning joggers suddenly trundled into view on
the path in front, both staring at the boat. Had they heard
something? Jamie took no chances. 'Morning! Wonderful day,
and a splendid garden!' he shouted, making a grab for the little
figurehead and popping at least twelve bubbles on its wrapping.
The athletes weakly waved back before staggering out of sight.

'A hasty over-reaction of yours,' muttered Nigriff, adjusting
his clothes. 'However,' he proudly announced, 'now at last you
will see the glory of Malplaquet!'

'This is your place, Nigriff – right?'

'A brilliant observation, sir – how did you know?'

'Call it an inspired guess. Come on, take me round.'

'Indeed, sir, I am honoured to show you this brave new world.
May I sit in the pocket behind your head?' Jamie gently placed
Nigriff in the hood of his jacket, then clambered out of the boat
onto the bank, one foot slipping off the muddy edge and into the
water. 'Do be careful!' shouted Nigriff in Jamie's ear. 'This is
our ever-flowing Stream of Consciousness! One should simply
listen, not splash about in it.'

'Listen?' asked Jamie.

'These noble waters spread understanding and insight to the
provinces, sir.' Nigriff spotted Jamie's puzzlement. 'Remember, even

your poets write of babbling brooks and murmuring streams.'

'Yes, but. . . .'

'And behold, the Cascade of Knowledge!' shouted the Elysian, as Jamie scrambled up the slope towards the waterfall. 'A torrent of inspiration!'

Jamie was careful not to put his other (dry) foot in the pool below the cascade, and then cast his eyes over Nigriff's province that lay before them; a small valley divided by a barely-moving river, with mature trees and bushes gathered around the grassy slopes and gentle hollows. It was beautiful, a quiet and soothing landscape.

'This is considered by those with good taste and judgement to be the oldest and the best of the provinces,' announced Nigriff grandly, with a touch of prejudice. 'Let me show you a selection of our heroes. Please walk round to the right.'

They stopped in front of a semi-circular wall displaying stone heads in niches; the inscriptions above showed they were kings, or people of great bravery or wisdom.

'I know these,' said Jamie over his shoulder to Nigriff. 'The British Worthies. Famous people in history – like Shakespeare here, or Queen Elizabeth, and King Alfred.'

'Indeed, sir. Men and women who deserve to be honoured in Elysium itself. They are our inspiration and example – and it may interest you to know, sir, that my extensive personal research has indicated that there could be close family ties between myself and at least twelve of these sixteen noble personages.'

'Only twelve, Nigriff?'

'My research is not yet complete. Unfortunately, the records are patchy on the remaining four, and I will have to resort to reasonable assumptions. Anyway, we must continue our perambulation, as there is much to see – the Shell Bridge, the Temple of Ancient Virtue. . . .'

At the end of the whole tour, beyond the Yews of Learning and back at the Cascade, Jamie looked again at the Worthies beyond the narrow strip of water. He was casually watching their upside-down reflections, when he realised to his amazement that the heads were moving slightly. They were turning sideways to look at their neighbours, nodding slowly, and smiling, possibly even talking to one another. He stood there, spellbound by the sight. But as soon as he raised his eyes from the watery images to the busts themselves, they all froze, becoming the usual line of stone heads in their own arches, staring blankly and impassively forward.

Jamie was shocked, but decided not to tell anybody for the moment. How could he possibly say he'd seen some old stone heads having a chat? Anyway, Nigriff interrupted his thoughts. 'Come, sir, it is time to return to Granny.' They picked their way back down the bank to their craft.

'Hang on, what about the fourth province?' said Jamie, determined to get a full tour, as he settled himself in the boat and reached for the oars.

'Ah yes, the Grecian Valley, where you had your recent picnic. A visit won't be necessary, sir; you have been there already.'

'I know the *place*, Nigriff, but not the *people*.'

'That's the best way to keep it, sir.' Jamie frowned at him; he was getting fed up with Nigriff's lack of interest in the other areas. Nigriff gave in. 'Oh, if you insist. They're soldiers, military types. What else need I say?'

Plenty more, thought Jamie, but knew he wasn't going to get any further. That left him one option. 'Tell you what, Nigriff, I'll give you a lift back, then I'm going for a walk by myself.'

'Of course, sir. To anywhere in particular?'

'Yes. The Grecian province,' said Jamie firmly.

'By yourself? Again?' Nigriff was alarmed. 'Do you think that's wise, sir? That valley is the final frontier, the very *edge* of our world!'

Jamie ignored his fussing. 'Come on, Nigriff. It wasn't exactly wild at the picnic. And the Grecian army's there – I'm sure they'll come to my help.'

'Come to your help, Master Jamie? They are the reason you will need help!' Nigriff was becoming agitated. 'They're savages, barbarians – this is utter madness!'

'Sorry, Nigriff. I'm thirteen now. A man's got to do what a man's got to do.'

The little Archivist just buried his head in his hands, quietly sighed, and another bubble exploded. Jamie smiled and headed the boat back across the lake.

An hour later Jamie was sat on the Grecian Temple steps, leaning back against a column and facing the shallow valley with its sunlit trees. He was on the lookout for tiny people. And he was thinking.

He was wondering whether the idea of descendants from the island of Lilliput living in an English Landscape Garden, wasn't just too weird to be true. After all, he'd only met one little person so far. And what would happen when the story got out? He could already see the headlines in the newspapers – 'Ancient Storybook Midgets Living in Garden.' It did sound ridiculous, and sitting up there all by himself, he was imagining his friends taking the mickey out of him.

Anyway, there was no point just sitting around. He decided to check out a path to his left. He began to get to his feet – but couldn't. His waist was stuck to the pillar.

Perhaps his trousers had got caught. He twisted round as best he could, and noticed some thin wires passing through his trouser belt-loops and right round the column. He pulled hard and fingered the wire but it was no use. He'd been tied up.

'Hey! Who's done this?' His shouts echoed back off the temple but received no reply. No reply that is, apart from the immediate appearance of two rats, in perfect step and with tiny plumes on their heads, pulling a small toy Jeep. Alone on the back seat, looking relaxed but attentive, was an imposing figure, wearing a dark military jacket with epaulettes, a large peaked cap, and with a stick under his left arm. A soldier in combat gear was at the wheel. 'Grecians!' thought Jamie. The small cavalcade stopped by his feet. The General slowly stood up and faced the prisoner. He spoke loudly and clearly.

'My name is General Thorclan, leader of the Grecian Army. I gather you are here to protect us. How are you managing so far?'

Jamie swallowed, and had the presence of mind to introduce himself politely – and not mention Borrowers.

He'd been tied up.

'Good afternoon, General Thorclan. I'm very pleased to meet you. Um . . . I'm a bit stuck at the moment. I might need your help.'

'Excellent summary of present position, young sir, we'll make a soldier of you yet.' He was helped out of the car by his driver, and then paced around Jamie. 'The lads from the Cobham Regiment have done a good job. Proper calibre of fishing line, and superb knots – especially that double transverse hitch with a running sheep bend. I *do* like that; definitely tied by a complete knotter.'

Jamie was wondering why they'd captured him. 'Am I your enemy, General?'

'Enemy? Goodness me, of course not, there aren't any left nowadays. Not *real* enemies – just the occasional pain in the rear end – right, Yenech?'

The driver agreed, with a smart salute and a snap of his heels.

'Well, if you're not fighting enemies, what do spend your time doing?' asked Jamie. 'Practising knots?'

'Training!' grunted Thorclan, with great enthusiasm. 'The boys love it – and so do the girls, I have to say.'

'But why do you train, if you never do any fighting?'

'Clearly you don't come from a military background, young man. There are standards, traditions, and most importantly the Inter-Provincial Games. They depend upon two central factors; supreme levels of fitness, teamwork, and last of all, intelligence. That's the most important one in my book.'

Jamie counted up and decided that the third needed working on. 'So are you training now?'

'Absolutely. Thought you'd never ask. Come in and see.' He pointed towards the pair of double doors of the Temple's main room. 'Follow me. We'll lift the bolt for you; loose vents are fine for us.'

'One problem,' said Jamie slowly. 'I can't move.'

'Problem solved – Yenech, the knife!' The driver took out from the vehicle a small penknife, probably once attached to a keyring. He offered it to Jamie, who cut the fishing line and handed back the weapon to Yenech. He saluted in gratitude, and proceeded to drive the General round the side of the building. 'Wait here!' shouted the old soldier on parting.

Within seconds, Jamie heard the scrape of a bolt being lifted on the inside of the left-hand door. He gingerly pulled it open and looked inside. The sight that greeted him was – well, a few days ago it would have been beyond belief. It was even now, after everything that had happened, still extraordinary.

The windowless room was well lit by electric bulbs high up on the walls, and in every area there was a flurry of activity and organised commotion. There must have been a couple of hundred members of the Grecian Army there, in groups of about fifteen or twenty, each being instructed by an older officer. A few briefly glanced at him, but the overall concentration on their tasks was impressive. Jamie remembered Nigriff's comment about how undisciplined Grecians were.

'I'm afraid I can't *personally* show you around the programme,' said Thorclan apologetically. 'I'm due to meet some cadets who have all passed their first Basic Training Day. Atrocious conditions, y'know – bright sunshine, big coach party, three loose dogs and, to cap it all, using a sub-standard squirrel.' He beckoned Jamie down towards him and whispered, 'One of those 'L'-Class Leapers, y'know, not really up to it any more, but some of my senior officers love 'em. Can't bear to see them replaced by the new 'B'-Class Bounders. . . . Anyway, I'll leave you with Yenech. Not a great soldier, but a superb driver, and a mine of information. I'll try to find you later.'

'Certainly, General, thank you very much.' *Try* to find me?' wondered Jamie. It won't be that hard. 'So Yenech, squirrels first?'

'Yes sir, over here, sir. Some younger officers are practising their starts.'

In one corner stood a line of three squirrels, tails curled up high behind their backs. Staff in blue overalls, presumably ground crew, technicians, and beauticians, were making final adjustments with towels and combs. A tanned and muscular soldier was walking along the line of trainees, giving them a seriously hard time.

'How many times have I told you? Settle in the seat *before* take-off! And where's the seat? *Between* the tail and his back. Any questions?'

He stopped in front of one soldier.

'Anidox! How can you hope to stay on sat like that? First steep turn and you're really flying – straight down!'

Anidox said nothing. The trainer carried on with his theme.

'I know – always wanted to fly squirrels, ever since you saw one leaping overhead. But you can't even *sit* on one! Troyal, make my day! Jump onto Walnut.'

Troyal briefly hesitated, looked at the other pilots, and then made a quick dash towards the nearest rodent. The squirrel seemed nervous, rightly so, because Troyal's final leap was badly aimed and caught the animal full on the side, knocking it to the ground. It lay there twitching and groaning for a while, before struggling back to its feet, rubbing its bruises.

'If that squirrel's out of action, *you* can carry your mates up the trees instead! Get back in line!' shouted the frustrated group leader.

There was clearly some progress still to be made.

'Some of this kit looks like Action Man stuff,' said Jamie.

'Correct, sir, but we cut it down to size, and the boots we melt into shape. Madam is our main supplier, car boot sales and the like, so it's usually old gear. We really want the new Space Exploration stuff – the round plastic helmet is perfect for our Deep Marsh Expeditions. The weapons don't work until our technicians adjust them – and not always after that. Well, not how they're meant to anyway.'

They were stepping past a section doing drill, and approaching a group with climbing ropes and grappling irons (to be accurate, bent safety-pins and fish-hooks). A team of twenty was being trained in the finer points of cliff-face attacks, helped by conspicuous blobs of chewing-gum on the smooth walls. The climbers were doing better than the squirrel pilots, until Jamie heard a shout; 'Don't put it in your mouth, Lylek, you've no idea where that's been – and it's the next handhold! Stick it back!'

Yenech and Jamie continued past one section being taught to

fence (with small toothpicks), and then finally met what Yenech described as 'the cream of the Grecian Army' – the archers.

'We've good supplies of arrows, with the honourable lady giving us her dressmaking pins, and bicycle clips make powerful crossbows. Our shooting will impress you, sir.'

The targets lined up against a wall two metres away intrigued Jamie – a Barbie doll with a moustache, a one-armed clown, a lego policeman and a plastic figure of a footballer kicking a ball and carrying a loose handbag.

'Extra points for the handbag,' explained Yenech. 'Our best can hit the policeman five times out of five in a cross-wind,' he added.

A volley of arrows was let off, and Jamie saw two figures mortally wounded and the policeman's hat knocked off. Yenech nodded with approval.

'That'll be Strenop – slow left-arm spin, prefers overcast conditions, but almost unplayable even indoors.'

Jamie remembered he had a job to do. 'I *do* need to speak to General Thorclan before I leave,' he said to Yenech. They wandered over to where he was standing by the doors.

'General, I know you said you haven't any enemies, but I *have* been given the task of protecting you. I want to prove I can do it.'

'As it happens, young sir, I have been thinking about what's the biggest nuisance around here, and it comes down to one thing – that Gratton fellow and his dog. We've tried everything over the years, and he's still at large. If you could stop Gratton, then we'd be right behind you.'

'No problem,' said Jamie instantly. 'Actually, what *is* the problem?'

'What are his main weapons, Yenech?' said the General.

'RLBMs, sir.'

'Standing for?'

'Racket Launched Ball Missile, sir.'

'Exactly. Fellow's a wretched pain – goes out everyday with his massive black dog, Hobbes, and bashes tennis balls with an ancient racket. Absolutely lethal; no sense of direction, no warning, plenty of injuries amongst my men. Huge dog lumbers into the bushes, knocks 'em over, and licks them senseless. That's your mission, Jamie, should you choose to accept it. Can you stop these brutes?'

'Easy, General Thorclan, I've got a plan.'

'Brilliant; let's put a time-scale on it. 5pm, in two days time. See you soon.'

Jamie walked out, closed the doors behind him, and then leaned back against them. How could he stop a teacher at Malplaquet School from exercising his dog?

But he had to, otherwise he'd never be an Assistant Guide for the Lilliputians.

This was his first and possibly biggest test.

Fail, and it would be over before he'd started.

4: The First Battle

Seated in her favourite comfy chair, Granny was half-hidden behind the large pages of the Financial Times, and mumbling to herself. 'Half-yearly report for Pills4U Medicals, getting much better. Hmm, little change in PocketMoney.Com . . . , South Sea Baubles expanding rapidly. . . . PizzaFirst rising slowly. . . .' Nigriff was standing on a window-sill, admiring his reflection in the glass, straightening his clothes and turning from side to side, when he suddenly spotted Jamie coming through the gate, looking very pleased with himself.

'Hi, you two,' said the newcomer cheerily, entering the sitting-room. 'Well, that wasn't too bad.' The colour drained from Nigriff's face.

Granny put down her glasses and the paper. 'Oh good, I was hoping you'd be back soon. Apparently you wanted to stretch your legs after the maiden voyage.' Nigriff was nervously wringing his hands. The old lady continued. 'And what wasn't too bad?'

Jamie came straight out with it. 'Seeing the Grecians. I met General Thorclan, and watched his men training. They were fine – really nice to me. Not what I . . . ' and he paused, glancing at Nigriff, 'had . . . expected.'

'Of course they were fine, just like the others. And what did you think of the Cascadians?' Jamie hesitated, so Granny carried on. 'Did you see their new boatyards, by the Cascade?' 'Well . . . it was, um . . . ' Jamie was floundering.

Nigriff helped out. 'Time was short, Madam, it was a question of . . . ' Granny held up her hand to stop him. 'Nigriff, I *don't* believe it. And I suppose you didn't see many Palladians either?'

Silence.

'But you had a detailed tour of every nook and cranny of Elysium. Correct?'

Nigriff was panicking, and the words came out all wrong. 'Madam, not *every* crook and nanny, I mean crack and noony, no, nack and . . . oh dear.' He swallowed hard and waited for the telling-off.

The old lady didn't disappoint him. 'Nigriff, this just *won't* do. You had specific instructions to show Jamie *everything* – how can it work if you miss out so much?'

Jamie noticed her words. 'How can what work?' he thought. Time to find out some more – and to help Nigriff out.

'Granny, Nigriff *did* want to tell me about other parts, like the Japanese Gardens – but he said it was far better coming from you.' Nigriff threw him a weak smile of gratitude.

'Hmm. Is that right? Well, they are *very* important, so perhaps I'd better.' She settled back down in her chair. 'You remember I told you the Lilliputians first hid on the island on the Eleven-Acre? Well, just before it was taken apart, they all migrated to the Japanese Gardens. The then owner of Malplaquet had built a special model city for them, not just with houses, but also with schools, shops and even watchtowers. And, would you believe it, even their own railway network – the most wonderful Hornby layout.'

'Hang on a minute,' interrupted Jamie. 'So he knew about the people? He could see them?'

'Correct,' acknowledged Granny. 'From childhood.'

'Did people come and see the model city?'

'Of course – funnily enough, it was the best way to hide the tiny folk. Awfully cunning.' She laughed to herself, and then explained that the public had been allowed to come every Friday, paying one shilling, with proceeds to the Red Cross. On that day the townspeople had hidden elsewhere, but there had been stiff penalties for any Lilliputian who had left a bed unmade – which might have attracted suspicion. 'As far as I know, nobody ever realised there were tiny people living in the little buildings.'

Nigriff added some more information, to show Granny that he was willing to discuss other areas of the gardens. 'It will come as no surprise to you, sir, when I say that the model city was later dismantled. There are no traces of it left.'

'Not again!' said Jamie. 'First Lilliput . . . then the island in the lake . . . then this city. Do all the places they live in disappear?'

'It does sound strange, sir, and it has been most inconvenient. It has made it particularly difficult for the Lilliputians to understand their history.'

'So did the four provinces begin when they left the model city?'

'Indeed, sir, in the period called the Great Divergence.'

'But why did they leave?'

'Sadly the owner had been too extravagant – money was short, and there was no alternative but to sell up. The mansion of Malplaquet became a school, and the Lilliputians had to scatter and hide in the grounds.'

Jamie noticed Granny looking sadder by the minute. As he stopped to think about it, it was a sorry tale; little people always on the move, with nowhere they could really call home. The old lady took a deep breath and added, 'What's especially upsetting is that nowadays, as Nigriff said, they have no idea about their origins, about Lilliput. Absolutely no idea at all.' She sniffled.

Nigriff agreed. 'We have old stories, of course, about once living on a beautiful island, but they are regarded as ancient myths, not proper history.'

'They've really no idea where they come from?'

'Quite right, sir.'

'I do think you can help with that, Jamie,' added Granny. 'To tell them about their wonderful past. It'll be a big job, mind.'

'But I can't do it yet,' said Jamie. 'The Grecians have asked me to do a job for them.'

'What's that?'

'To get rid of a teacher and his dog.'

'Madness!' interrupted Nigriff. 'Typical of the Grecians. I did warn you, sir.'

Granny held up her hand for quiet. 'Have those two really become such a threat?'

'Sort of. He hits tennis-balls everywhere and the Grecians are getting hit.'

'Do you have a plan?'

'Not exactly – but I've got two days yet.'

In stark contrast to Nigriff (who was sulking), Granny was delighted about the task that Jamie had been set. 'This is *excellent* news. In spite of everything, you've made contact with one of the provinces, gained their trust, *and* been asked to help them. Just what the Assistant Guide should be doing. Nigriff, are you listening?'

'Yes, Madam,' came the gloomy reply. 'Listening *and* thinking.'

Day: the second of the two that Jamie had been allowed.
Plan: not yet decided.
Time: after lunch.
Hours left: three (plus stoppage time for injuries).
Jamie had been wandering round the grounds all morning and had thought up three possible plans.

Plan A (code-name *Dog Tired*), had occurred to him whilst sat in front of the Temple of Venus in Cascadia.
Cunning Tactics: gather up each tennis ball before Hobbes can find it.
Optimistic Result: Gratton realises his dog is too old and gives up.
Big Problem: Gratton might enjoy watching Hobbes compete with a boy, and thus fire off dozens more. Casualties enormous.
Likely Success: nil

Plan B (code-name *Mad Dog*); a brainwave on the Shell Bridge in Elysium.

> **Cunning Tactics:** persuade Gratton that Hobbes has contracted a dangerous form of canine insanity called 'Mutts' (Mixed-Up Tennis Teaching Syndrome).
> **Optimistic Result:** Gratton stops out of concern for his animal.
> **Big Problem:** Gratton already thinks his dog is stupid.
> **Likely success:** nil.
>
> *Plan C* (code-name *Doggone*).
> **Cunning Tactics:** arrange a holiday for Hobbes in the jungles of South-East Asia.
> **Optimistic Result:** dog gone.
> **Big Problem:** totally impractical.
> **Likely success:** less than nil.

Thus it had not been a great morning. The only thing to cheer him up had been Dad dropping his bike off while he was out. Mr. Thompson had apparently asked Granny how Jamie was doing; 'I told him you'd discovered lots of little things,' said Granny later. 'Well, that's true, isn't it?'

He was on his bike now, on the way to the Grecian province, and wondering where his brilliant idea was going to come from. In front of the Pebble Alcove he braked hard. Remembering the earlier misty pictures of the seashore, he couldn't help thinking that it might show him another lot of images. Anyway, he had nothing to lose by popping in briefly.

He lay his bike down on the grass, settled himself on the bench inside, and looked for any patterns to do with taking dogs for a walk. There was nothing obvious, but he found a wheel, or perhaps a circle, that with a bit of imagination could well be a tennis ball.

That would do. He stared hard at it.

The mist curtain dropped just as before, and on it he saw a crowd of people walking alongside a very long cart – a huge plank on wheels, like a giant skateboard, maybe thirty metres in length. They were all cheering and, even though again the language was unfamiliar, they were clearly very happy. Jamie tried to make out what was on the cart. It was a large shape tied down by ropes – in fact he realised it was a huge man, wearing old-fashioned clothes, and lying on his back. 'Good grief!' shouted Jamie, 'Gulliver!' As soon as he had uttered the word, the scene on the mist immediately faded, and he was simply looking out of the Alcove at the usual lake.

Trembling, he stood up, completely puzzled. Why should he see a picture of Gulliver? Because the story had been on his mind? This building was starting to give him the creeps.

He glanced down at his watch and with dismay saw that it was half-past two; Gratton would be taking Hobbes for his afternoon walk! He leapt on his bike, pedalled furiously across the Palladian Bridge, and bounced through Elysium towards the Grecian Valley. Then, even though his mind was in turmoil, he devised yet another cunning plan. Not a brilliant one – and his parents wouldn't approve – but it *might* just work. He pedalled even harder.

Mr. Gratton was in a very positive mood that afternoon. It was now two weeks into the summer holidays, and he had reached that wonderful point when all his old papers and documents from last term had been filed away (in his bin), and he had completed the necessary phone-calls and letters. Jobs done, he could relax by taking Hobbes for a spot of his usual Field Tennis.

He was searching round his porch. 'Darling, have you seen Old Faithful?' he called to his wife.

'Hobbes?'

'No, he's just *old*. I want the thing I hit them with.'

'Your cane? You can't use that anymore.'

'I know,' he answered crossly, and whispering to himself, 'Don't know what the world's coming to.' He kept searching. 'No, I mean the tennis racket.'

'It should be where it always is.'

'Well it isn't. Someone's moved it. I'll have to find another.' Gratton opened his store-cupboard in his study, peered in and then smiled. He'd forgotten about that one; a beautifully crafted racket, confiscated during the term for 'being used in an inappropriate way.' Made of a new lightweight alloy with a frightening whip to it, the name '*Terminator*' was emblazoned in black and gold letters on the shaft. 'This is more like it,' he said to himself. 'This should get the old beast moving. I'm going to enjoy myself.'

From their vantage point on the roof of the Grecian Temple, General Thorclan and a handful of troops were keeping a careful eye on proceedings. They had seen Jamie arrive on his bike round the back of Gratton's house, and had been impressed as he had nipped inside the porch and emerged with the old racket.

'Hmm, cunning plan,' mused the General, 'nicking the enemy's weapons. Can't deny the kid has guts – and brains. Could be our new secret weapon. Now, all I've got to do is find Yenech again.'

He turned his binoculars towards the trees, and panned round. He had sent out a small contingent as usual on guard duty that afternoon.

'General!' shouted Captain Trimter, one of the officers watching the teacher's residence. 'Gratton has selected another weapon. It looks like. . . . Oh my goodness, it's a Terminator!'

'I thought they'd been banned,' murmured Thorclan. 'I hope young Master Thompson knows what he's up against.'

Jamie had felt bad about sneaking round to Gratton's back door, but he'd reckoned that he wasn't *stealing* the offensive weapon, just borrowing it – just until Hobbes was exercised in other ways.

It was only when he was back across the valley that he saw the man leaving with the dreaded replacement. Jamie had immediately recognised it as a Terminator; the best tennis-player at his school used one, and his serves were unplayable, the balls flaring like a comet as they hurtled past. This was not good news.

Jamie knew something had to go. Removing another racket would be difficult, removing a large dog even more so (especially on a bike in broad daylight), and removing Gratton sounded illegal. That left one option.

The balls.

So for the next ten minutes, Jamie chased on his bike after every ball that Gratton hit into the bushes or trees. He usually got there well before Hobbes, because fortunately the new racket was belting them much further than ever before. The sad dog had to return empty-pawed to face the creative insults of its angry master.

'This is definitely working,' thought Jamie, out of breath after all his exertions. He was watching Gratton plod home after the loss of the final ball. 'Game, set and match,' he whispered confidently.

Horatius Gratton, the frustrated owner of an incompetent and knackered Flat-coated Retriever called Hobbes, kicked his back door open, and yelled upstairs. 'Never lost so many balls in my life. Where's that large bag?'

'Sorry, *who*?'

'That bag of balls, the ones the Groundsmen pick up. Hobbes needs another hour, he's totally unfit.' He bent down under a low shelf and shouted, 'Don't worry, found them.' He swung the net bag over his shoulder, and strode out, Hobbes panting along behind, his head hung low.

Dismay was spreading among the Grecian troops on the roof.

'*Massive* increase in firepower, sir. Huge bag full of missiles.'

'Use the mirror, Captain,' ordered Thorclan grimly. 'Tell the troops to stay undercover.' He was very unhappy. Jamie's plan wasn't working, and his men were now in even greater danger. A signaller held up a large chunk of mirror, and catching the sun's rays, flashed off coded messages to the ground troops.

And where was Yenech? Thorclan had made visual contact with all the others except him; once again his own driver was nowhere to be seen.

Jamie saw Gratton re-emerge, armed to the teeth and ready to do battle. Sadly, he watched as the huge figure took up position in the flat bottom of the valley. To Jamie's horror, he then began to loosen up, swinging his long arms and doing a few stretching exercises. 'This guy's deadly serious,' he thought. 'He just never gives up.'

Feeling defeated, he slowly cycled along the path through the trees on the upper slopes, realising that his protecting days were already over.

He had failed. Knocked out in the first round.

Gratton was having the time of his life. Balls were being fired off in every direction. '*This* is a man's sport,' he mused. 'Forget swimming – I'll look after the school tennis team instead.' He walloped one halfway down the valley. 'Terrific – never knew I could hit the ball so well! Got to be 80 metres. Now,' he said, looking up, 'there's a challenge. Never made the top of that slope yet. But today. . . .' His arms began to gyrate like a hairy windmill in slow motion. Then, taking in deep mouthfuls of air, he was ready to launch The Big One.

'Now, how do they do it at Wimbledon? Fierce stare, knees bent, slow build-up, toss in the air, arch the back, loud grunt and . . . . Pow! Fantastic – going like a rocket!'

'Sir, we've spotted Yenech. On the path at the top of the slope – but Gratton's seen him – he's launching an assault!'

'Do everything you can to warn him, soldier! Keep that mirror flashing; send the signal, '*Once more to the Beech*'!'

As Jamie cycled along the path, he was totally pre-occupied with how he might have done things differently. Suddenly, beyond his handlebars, he spotted a small figure, dressed in combats, standing in a small hollow in the path, transfixed by the sight of a bike bearing down on him.

'YENECH!' screamed Jamie, pulling hard on the brakes and leaning back and sideways. The bike slid from under him on the earthen path, and he fell to the ground with a heavy thump and clatter of metal. Partly winded by the fall, he lifted himself on one elbow to see if he had flattened the little fellow. Fortunately he hadn't; Yenech was standing some distance away, white as a sheet, but intact. As Jamie was looking up, flashes of sunlight caught him full in the face, almost blinding him, and he put his hands up to shield his eyes.

'General, it's Jamie, coming from those trees! He's trying to intercept the missile!'

'The boy's a hero – or a fool,' responded Thorclan. 'He's no idea of the force of those things.'

Jamie had a very good idea of their force – a tennis-ball had just thumped into his stomach, winding him badly, and leaving him doubled-up and gasping. Within seconds a large Flat-coated and insulted Retriever had staggered up the hill, determined to find this particular ball and win this final rally. Hobbes found its opponent lying defenceless and breathless, so the victorious dog stood over him, panting and grinning, blocking out the sun and dripping saliva onto the face below.

The Grecians had cheered wildly as they had seen Jamie get in the way of Gratton's fearsome serve, but their delight had subsided once they realised that Jamie had been wounded – and that the dog itself had moved in for the final assault. There was total silence on the roof of the temple. Their champion was powerless – and Gratton himself was striding up the hill to administer the coup de grâce.

Jamie was lying on his back, his eyes shut and his face wet with sweat and canine drips, waiting for the inevitable. It soon came.

'What on earth do you think you're doing?' yelled a familiar voice. 'Stupid animal! Get off him immediately!'

Jamie gingerly opened his eyes, and found that a long, black and menacing hairy face had been replaced by a round, red and unattractive bald one. It was speaking to him as well. 'I'm terribly sorry. I can't apologise enough.' Jamie was helped to his feet by an outstretched hand. 'Are you alright? I had no idea you were up here. Look, I think your bike's fine – are you okay? Did I hit you?'

Jamie found his voice again. 'Not really – I think I got in the way.'

'Don't be ridiculous. It's entirely my fault – the wrong place to play with something as powerful as this racket, and with a dog as stupid as Hobbes,' he added, looking at the crestfallen animal. 'The Sports Field's probably the best place.'

Jamie latched onto this. 'Brilliant idea, sir. Much more space for him to run around in, and it's over the frontier. . . , I mean, the *front here*, or the back I suppose . . . and it's a long way from the Grecians . . . I mean *Greeks* . . . tourists you know, might be

French, any country really. . . .'

Gratton stared at him. 'Are you sure you're not concussed? Shouldn't you get your head checked out?'

But Jamie just grinned, grabbed Gratton's hand, shook it enthusiastically, and jumped wildly up and down, waving in the direction of the Grecian Temple. Then he leapt on his bike, and pedalled happily away along the track, leaving Gratton scratching his head in puzzlement. And even above the sound of his scrunching wheels, Jamie thought he could hear the sound of some faint cheering from a nearby temple rooftop.

5: The Challenge in the Gothic Temple

Jamie was given a hero's welcome as he bounced up the steps of the Grecian Temple, to be greeted at the top by General Thorclan, who took hold of his right ankle in a firm hug. Numerous battalions and regiments were applauding and cheering, and even the squirrels were thrilled, their tails twirling madly in delight.

The champion was led inside and seated on a green camouflage sheet (one of Granny's old towels, thought Jamie). The army swarmed around him. The General, standing above them on an upturned cup, lifted his arms for silence and spoke first.

'Young Master, this is a glorious moment.' (Loud cheers) 'We have long hoped to see this day, but never believed that a human would bring it about. [Murmurs of agreement] Your victory is truly remarkable. [More loud cheers] On behalf of the Grecian province, I should like to propose a toast. Please take a cup of our own special vintage, Malplaquet Reserve!'

The drinks were handed round, mostly in acorn-shells, and Jamie was handed his in an egg-cup. He sniffed the red liquid; it had a fine aroma, smelling remarkably similar to blackberry juice. Thorclan reached the climax of his speech.

'Ladies and Gentlemen, please raise your cups. I give you Jamie, the Liberator of the Grecian province! Three cheers to our Protector!'

The assembled multitude raised their drinks, repeated the toast, and gave the required long and loud cheers.

'And now,' demanded Thorclan, again asking for silence, and looking at Jamie in admiration, 'now you must tell us how you did it.'

Nigriff was back at Granny's in a mild state of shock. 'In all honesty, Madam, I don't know how he did it. One moment he was cycling away, utterly demoralised, and the next moment Gratton *himself* was offering a sincere apology and admitting defeat. Remarkable.'

Unbeknown to Jamie, Nigriff had spied the epic encounter from under a nearby bush, and had been so excited at the finale that he had actually run all the way back to the cottage. (This had caused such a stir en route, that mothers had brought their children out to see the sight. Many years later, they still remembered what they were doing, 'On the day that Nigriff ran.')

'Well, Nigriff, this shows the calibre of the boy. Our confidence in him is well-founded,' replied the old lady, delighted with the success of her protégé.

'Indeed, Madam, but it was the *manner* of his victory that was so astonishing. He seemed to encourage Gratton to bring out his biggest weapon. And let us not forget that he saved the life of a Grecian in the process. Again I say, remarkable.'

Granny agreed. 'Things are turning out wonderfully well. As I keep saying, Nigriff, he's definitely the one.'

Nigriff couldn't share her delight. 'I know you will think me cautious, Madam, but I'm only being, well, cautious. There are two recent events that are causing me considerable anxiety.'

Granny raised one eyebrow.

'Let me explain. First, I suspect that before defeating Gratton, the young master entered the Pebble Alcove. I saw him pedalling *furiously* away from there, looking alarmed. I believe something of a dramatic nature happened to him in there.'

Granny raised the other eyebrow.

Nigriff continued. 'I must repeat, Madam, my long-held belief that deep within the fabric of that building lie unknown forces. The evidence is becoming more compelling as each day passes.'

Granny lowered both eyebrows and shook her head. 'I *know* what you think, Nigriff, but I just can't see how an old building can have 'strange powers' whizzing around inside it. It doesn't make any sense.'

Nigriff decided, for the time being, to move on to his other point.

'Secondly, and equally seriously, Madam, do you remember that old manuscript I once showed you, that perhaps described the new Empire? It mentioned the *Forces of Restoration* and the *Forces of Destruction* – good things and bad things both becoming stronger. We may well be at the start of that process.'

'What makes you think so, Nigriff?' asked Granny, shifting in her chair.

'It happened at the Rotunda this morning, only minutes after the gardens opened. He must have been the first one in.'

'Who was, Nigriff? Who are you talking about?'

'A gentleman, if that is fitting for one so shabbily dressed, whom I spotted there. He was loitering around, and carrying a large folder, open at a picture of the Rotunda. I didn't like his manner. I was particularly concerned when he bent down and began to tap the steps and the base of the columns. I fear he was seeking traces of our ancient habitation.'

'Nigriff, do you know who *I* think he was?' Granny was speaking calmly, no longer troubled.

'You *know* his identity, Madam?'

'He'll just be a National Trust architect, or an historical assistant. They check restored buildings, making sure the work's done properly. That's all he was doing.'

Nigriff wasn't convinced. 'I wish I could say that your words have reassured me, Madam, but they haven't. He didn't seem at all trustworthy. I believe I can recognise a good historian when I see one.'

'So can I, Nigriff, and there's one right in front of me. Look, we both know that things are changing, so we can't be sure about what happens next.' Nigriff shrugged his shoulders, but continued to listen. 'But we can be sure about this; Jamie has gained the confidence of one province. That was an important first step for him. His next is to persuade the other three of his suitability.'

'In that case, Madam, he will need to get a motion passed in the Provincial Assembly. There's no other way.'

'Absolutely right, Nigriff – and we both know how easy that will be. Another test for our fine young man.'

'And should we show him the prophecy soon? To encourage him perhaps?'

'No, I don't think so, Nigriff. He needs to actually prove himself in the field – or I should say the gardens? It should be an interesting few days. . . .'

After his talk to the troops about his first mission, Jamie was now speaking privately to General Thorclan. He had described the events honestly to the men, but the Grecians had ignored words such as 'accidentally,' or 'surprisingly'. To their mind, Jamie had conducted a campaign of brilliant strategy and stunning tactics. They took his version as an indication of his humility, superb soldiering, and moral strength. The whole account, henceforth known as 'Gratton's Final Delivery,' was written up and became a central part of the course for Officer Training (Book 5: *Famous Battles*, Section 1(d) 'Inspired Tactics Against Overwhelming Odds').

Thorclan had been discussing with Jamie their respective future roles. Jamie had declined his generous offer to become Supreme Commander, saying that being an Assistant Guide was quite enough, thank you for asking anyway. Instead, he argued, why shouldn't Thorclan and his army defend all *four* of the provinces?

That suggestion left the General speechless. He eventually expressed the opinion that, with the greatest respect, Jamie hadn't been around long enough to realise that they didn't trust each other.

'I *do* realise that, General. That's why it's a good idea – you'll get on better.'

'But this is a huge change, sir, and excuse my impertinence, but haven't *you* been asked to be our Protector? And you *are* very good at it.'

'General Thorclan, my job is partly to protect you, but also to help the people protect themselves. We *must* persuade the other provinces to let the Grecians defend them.'

'Personally, sir, I suspect your recent victory may have confused your brain. Believe me, I know exactly what it's like. But if you insist, you must outline a proposal in the Provincial Assembly.'

'The what?'

'That's the tricky bit, sir. Let me explain.'

Jamie arrived back at Granny's house in the early evening, still light enough for her to see his clothes covered in grass stains and streaks of dirt.

'Goodness me, just look at you! What would your mother say?'

'Er, what about 'Hello'?' guessed Jamie.

'More likely something about a hosepipe. . . . Come on, shower before supper – and then you can tell me what you've been up to – or down in!'

Over supper Jamie outlined the glorious details of 'Gratton's Final Delivery.' It was only later when he was sat up in bed, and she came to say goodnight, that he felt able to talk about anything else.

'Granny, there's a couple of other things.'

'Go on.'

'Well, there's the Pebble Alcove.'

'What about it?' asked Granny, sitting down and trying not to react. She was only too aware of Nigriff's ideas about it.

'You know I told you about those images of people on the beach? Before I beat Gratton, I went in again and got a really clear picture of Gulliver.'

'G . . . G . . . Gulliver?' she stuttered. This was dramatic news. 'Are you sure?'

'Definitely, that bit early on when he's tied up on a long trolley. It was weird.'

Granny fell silent and then regained her composure. 'I, um, wouldn't worry about that too much, Jamie. The book's been on your mind; one of the pebble patterns probably made you think about him. Now, what else was it?'

Jamie could see that she was deliberately changing the subject, but he was too tired to find out why. 'Oh yes; the Provincial Assembly. Is it as bad as they say?'

'It depends. Why do you ask?'

'Thorclan's taking me to the next session. I'm proposing that the Grecian army defend all the provinces. I wouldn't need to run around everywhere, and they might all get on better.'

'Absolutely right, Jamie,' beamed the old lady. 'That's been my hope for years – it was *such* a shame when they went their separate ways. Now, let me explain; the Assembly is like their government, the only time when they formally meet together. All four provinces send representatives, and each province can usually propose one motion each session. . . .' Her voice began to drone on about how it was organised.

Within seconds the exertions of the day got the better of Jamie; our new hero relaxed back on his pillow and drifted off into a well-earned sleep.

Two days later in the early evening, Jamie was walking up the hill with Thorclan and three other Grecians towards the Gothic Temple, the seat of the Provincial Assembly. It was an eerie building – all pointed edges, sharp windows and open turrets. It would suit a horror film, thought Jamie, especially at Halloween in the dusk. You could easily imagine bats fluttering around, and thin ghostly faces peering out of the windows.

The ground-plan of the Temple was a triangle, with a tower on each point. As they walked through the door, Jamie saw that the large single room in the middle went up through both storeys. In the centre of its floor was a circular rug.

'Just like King Arthur,' whispered Thorclan discreetly, 'and the Knights of the Round Table – good soldiers by the way. The circle stops any province from being top. Some clever chap called these sessions the *Nights of the Round Carpet.*'

'So who's in Arthur's place?' asked Jamie, looking at a female Lilliputian seated on a square stone.

'That's the Listener,' replied Thorclan. 'She oversees the Assembly, and makes sure that everything happens properly and fairly. We have a different one every ten moons – this one's Vingal. She's a Grecian – but don't expect any favours.'

All the other Provincial Representatives (PRs) had been settling themselves down cross-legged along a green circle running just inside the edge of the rug. Thorclan told Jamie to sit behind on the tassels; 'You're a fringe member.'

The session began with a rather odd display by Perditrag (a Cascadian PR), of what Thorclan described as 'stick-leaping' – a series of dramatic and tortuous movements with a small cane. 'Particularly good one, that,' acknowledged the General when it was over.

'Why do they do it?' asked Jamie, very bemused.

'No idea,' admitted Thorclan, 'goes back a long way, I think.'

Events moved rapidly on. Jamie was officially and warmly welcomed by the Listener, who summarised his exploits and also his role as the new respected Assistant Guide to Granny. This was followed by some equally polite greetings from a number of other PRs. Jamie felt that this body was behaving in a most sensible and mature way, and so looked forward to some intelligent debate. The first motion was then announced; '*More Sport on the Provincial Schools' Timetable.*' A Cascadian PR stood up to propose it.

'Madam Listener, I'm sure we all agree. . . .'

'Not a chance, Yamlack, we've heard it all before!' shouted Stronbore, a dark-haired Palladian woman with a clear voice.

'Order! Let the honourable gentleman finish!' rejoined the Listener.

'Absolutely, dearest lady, that's what we'd all like!' (Humelish, Grecian)

'Order!'

'Madam, as I was saying, the timetable in our schools is dominated by too many academic subjects. . . .'

'A point of information,' (Sivad, Elysian), 'it's logically impossible to have *too many* academic subjects.' (Loud cheers and stamping of feet from Elysians). 'I would ask the Cascadian PR to withdraw his last sentence.'

'Was that his *last* sentence?' (Thorclan, Grecian) 'Or is that just wishful thinking?'

'ORDER!' barked Vingal the Listener, really getting into her stride. 'We haven't heard the proposal yet. Let the man speak.'

'I would like to remind the Assembly,' said an elegant Elysian lady, Sheketh by name, 'that we had to listen to this very same proposal at our previous meeting.'

'No, we didn't,' complained Yamlack, 'I didn't get this far last time.'

'Can I propose,' continued the Elysian, 'that we submit this proposal to a vote? It would be the most rational way forward.'

'Agreed,' accepted Madam Listener happily. 'Please consider your responses.'

'What happens now?' whispered Jamie, leaning towards Thorclan.

'It's a question of Eyes or Nose. If you think you can see something good about the proposal, then you make two rings over your eyes with your fingers – like this.' And he made two circles as if he was wearing glasses. 'But if you think the proposal stinks, you hold your nose.'

'Responses!' snapped the Listener. One set of PRs made circles around their eyes, and three sets held their noses.

'The Noses have it,' she announced. 'Brief recess. Elysian proposal next.'

'That was lucky,' said Thorclan enthusiastically, turning round towards Jamie. 'Your very first Assembly and you hear a first-class debate.'

'First-class?' responded Jamie in astonishment.

'Absolutely,' replied Thorclan. 'I lost count of the number of people that spoke. About half the Representatives I should think.'

'But we didn't get to hear his ideas.'

'Yes we did – he wanted more sport in our schools.'

'But he hardly said anything!'

'*Hardly said anything*?' replied Thorclan, in surprise. 'He spoke on at least three occasions – two more than last time! I know what you're thinking,' he continued, 'I'm sure things are done *very* differently in your world.' (Jamie knew that one would never find such antics in the House of Commons). 'We won't agree on anything – so we get on and vote quickly. It saves lots of time.'

'Doesn't give me much hope, does it?'

'Oh, I don't know. There's always an outside chance.' Thorclan turned back to face the centre as the Elysians' turn was announced.

Ten minutes later and there was only one proposal left. The

Elysians hadn't got very far with their idea that a recently-discovered logical puzzle, called a Rubik's Cube, should be included in the Inter-Provincial Games. The Palladian Tultnoc brothers had said that they would only accept it as part of the Construction Events, and the Cascadians had complained that it wouldn't float properly, and anyway it was entirely the wrong shape for any Sports Event.

The Palladians had fared even less well. When they had made the novel suggestion that they should give courses in 'Communication by Whistling,' they had received lots of whistles in reply. 'We're pretty good at it already,' jeered a Cascadian, 'so sit down!'

'Finally for this session, the Grecian proposal!' announced the Listener, pleased with the civilised behaviour so far.

'Over to you, young sir,' murmured Thorclan. 'They won't mind if you don't stand up. Probably best that way.'

'Madam Listener, and honourable members of the Assembly,' Jamie began, still seated, and trying his best to sound confident and important. 'I'd like to thank you for your earlier warm welcome.' He was pleased to see that he had their attention – and that he was being allowed to start a second sentence. 'I have been most impressed with the quality of your debates this evening. It almost reminds me of our own parliament.' There were murmurs of approval, although Jamie did hear one voice growling, 'Get on with it!'

'The Grecian proposal is a simple one. That they should form the Defence Force for all four provinces, so that you and your families can live in greater safety.' There was silence – a shocked silence – and then a huge uproar broke out.

Once the Listener had restored a semblance of order, reminding the PRs of their honourable status, Jamie was asked to explain further. He spent some time outlining how the Grecians were seasoned professionals, with a huge experience of training. The plan would give the other provinces freedom to live as they wished, rather than spend time trying to protect themselves.

Jamie thought he was beginning to persuade one or two, but he was still dreading the vote. His role of Assistant Guide might be in doubt if he couldn't get this idea through the Assembly. After he had finished (and incidentally, it was the longest ever speech in the

And then a huge uproar broke out

history of the Provincial Assembly), he was relieved to hear the words of the lady in charge.

'It would be unusual to vote on a motion put forward by a fringe member, even if he is speaking for the Grecians. I am going to suggest something different; a compromise, and a challenge. We will see what this Grecian army is made of. Their reputation in training is satisfactory. We need to see them in actual conflict.'

Jamie saw Thorclan rubbing his hands in eager anticipation.

'My proposal is this,' she continued, her eyes scanning round the members. 'The Grecian Army, perhaps with the help of the new guide, should mount an offensive against the uncivilised hordes swarming over the South Front and Home Park. If they can force a retreat, we will vote on the motion at our next Assembly.'

There were many murmurs of approval at this wise conclusion to the session, which finished, as always, with the Listener calling, 'Time!' The PRs began to make their way home to their respective provinces. Jamie could hear the frantic buzz of their conversations, but he still wasn't clear about what was expected of himself and the Grecians.

Thorclan was in no doubt. 'This is the *big* one, Jamie, the one we've been training for.'

'But what does she want you to do? *Uncivilised hordes?* Does she mean the kids at the school?'

'No, of course not – they're no problem. It's those people with the long sticks and enormous wheeled chariots. The Golfers. She wants us to sort out the Golfers. This could be very messy. Exciting – but messy.'

6: The Golf War

Jamie hoped to meet with General Thorclan to plan the campaign against the entire membership of Malplaquet Golf Club, but suddenly there was no time. Granny announced her news as soon as he walked in the door.

'Jamie, your Mum's phoned; you have to go back first thing tomorrow. They've got a late booking for a holiday in France.'

'What? You're joking?'

'No, I'm not – you won't be around for a while.'

'But I can't go now,' groaned Jamie, 'there's going to be a war!'

'A war? What do you mean?' Granny replied, most alarmed.

'It's the golfers. The Assembly will only let the Grecians defend everyone if they can sort out the golfers. The Listener said they're all a complete menace.'

'I see,' said Granny, 'but it's probably just the Military Golfers.'

'The what?'

'The Military Golfers – Thorclan will explain. Anyway, it does sound as if you should stay. Let me have a think. Hmm . . . I wonder . . . that *might* work. . . .'

Mr. Thompson almost drove off the road when Jamie made a sudden and surprising admission. 'I've been having a great time at Malplaquet, Dad. Architecture and History are so interesting – you can learn lots in a landscape garden.' The astonished parent regained his concentration and seized this rare moment. 'I'm glad you think so. So what have you learnt?'

'Oh, let me think.' (What had Granny told him to say?) 'The different styles of architecture, y'know, the classical Grecian Temple, and the medieval, like the Gothic Temple.'

Mr. Thompson stopped the car to look across at his son, who was hoping his Dad wouldn't ask him anything too difficult. So Jamie got the next sentence in first. 'It's *such* a shame this holiday's got in the way.'

'Well, there's plenty of architecture in France,' came the reply. 'You could study that while we're there.'

Granny had seen that argument coming and had coached Jamie well. 'But it's not the same as ours, is it? And Malplaquet is Britain's Greatest Work of Art of the Georgian Period,' (Brilliant quote from the National Trust Guidebook). 'Can't I stop with Granny while you and Mum go? You could have some time by yourselves, and Charlie's got loads of friends – well, people he can stay with.' The 'time by yourself' argument was clever, very clever. Mr. Thompson easily weakened.

By the time they got home, Granny had already employed similar tactics on the phone with Mum. It was another easy victory. Mrs. Thompson had quickly accepted that a holiday in a French cottage with just her husband would be much, *much* more relaxing than with two adolescents as well. As for Charlie, he was certain that Jamie was up to something, but he preferred a week with his friend to days of autoroutes, medieval villages, and estate agents' windows. He'd work on Jamie another time.

So at the end of that day, Jamie was back at Malplaquet, having collected his computer, lots of books about British Architecture (to impress the parents), and stacks of paper, pens and sheets of cardboard. Thorclan arrived, and they drew a large map of Malplaquet, plotting the field of conflict. Squirrels were put on Orange Alert and a meeting of senior officers was called that same evening.

The Golf War was about to begin.

It was the early stages of the briefing. Jamie was sat on his bed with six high-ranking officers of the Grecian Army, facing the map of Malplaquet that was hanging on the wall. Just below it, on an old tiled washstand, stood Thorclan.

'As we thought, gentlemen, it's only the Military Golfers, not the whole army.'

'Sorry, General,' said Jamie, 'I don't understand.'

'They're awfully cunning blighters, Jamie. You can't predict the path of their white missiles – they go 'left, right, left, right,' to the target, rather than flying in a straight line. We're not safe anywhere, not even the long grass; in fact that's often their favourite landing-site. Anyway, let me introduce someone who can help us.'

He walked to the back of the washstand and called down. Two dirty hands appeared over the top, followed by a rugged and weather-beaten figure. Clothed in rough brown leather, his boots were dirty, and on his head squatted a fur cap.

Thorclan was pleased with himself. 'Gentlemen, we are most fortunate to find our leading explorer, Kryasp. He famously discovered the Stone of Jedaris in the far eastern lands, and has lived alone in the wilds occupied by strange types like gardeners, fishermen – and the golfers. I can safely say there is *no-one* more qualified to explain their tactics and cunning. Kryasp, we look forward to your words.'

There was polite applause and then silence. Kryasp looked hard at them. They looked back. He leaned on his stick. He scratched his chin. He rubbed his shoulder. Then he spoke.

'Golfers.' He was chewing something in his mouth. 'Nasty.'

'Splendid,' enthused Thorclan, 'could you give us *slightly* more detail?'

He scratched his chin again. '*Very* nasty,' he grunted.

'Good, good. Now we're getting somewhere. What can you tell us, Kryasp, from all your years of contact with these people?'

The great outdoors man looked bemused. He pondered the question. He thought of an answer, and then decided against it. Finally, after a bit more chewing, he spoke.

'Golfers?' he queried. 'Stay away from 'em.'

With that he climbed over the back of the washstand and disappeared.

'Well, that gives us a useful start,' beamed Thorclan, 'a precise description of character and one proposed set of tactics.'

'Sir, I may be able to help further,' interjected a young fresh-faced officer, leaping to his feet. 'I've made a special study of their strategy.'

'Could be helpful, Cherbut. Fire away.'

The officer cleared his throat and began his briefing. 'They're unlike other soldiers, sir; they don't like using their ammo. The fewer shots they take, the happier they are. Our logical strategy, therefore, is to weaken their morale by making them shoot too much.'

'So are you saying that if they use *lots* of shots, they may not fight again?'

'*Exactly*, sir, hole in one – if you see what I mean, sir.'

'Brilliant. This is most encouraging. And their armaments? Any details?'

'Not what you would expect, sir. They have two types of missile launchers – wood and iron. The 'woods', as they call them, can send a missile skimming not far above ground level at frightening speeds for vast distances. The iron launchers aren't a lot safer; their missiles can reach an extraordinary height, and then can land on you without warning out of the sun. They even have special irons for the desert areas. These launchers are now transported in fully motorised carriers, not pulled by hand like in the old days.'

Thorclan winced. 'Good grief, what will they think of next? And what about their missiles?'

'A cunning design. The inner core contains the explosive power, and the hard outer core produces the deadly impact. There are a whole series of missiles – for different weather conditions, of various colours according to the terrain, and also special types for men and women to fire. They even have ones that glow in the dark; we defused one they lost two nights ago.'

Thorclan was realising what they were up against. 'Gentlemen,' he said, turning to his staff, 'we cannot fight on all fronts at once.'

He struck areas on the map with his stick. 'If we can hit the enemy hard in these Sectors – 4, 5, 6, 7, and 8 – then 1, 2, 3, and 9 may also fall. I'm convinced this is our best hope of victory.'

Thorclan continued the briefing for another hour. Officers were assigned their Sectors, and troops and weaponry were discussed. Jamie was impressed. Thorclan drew the meeting to a close.

'Gentlemen, thank you for your patience. It has been a long but productive session. I am fully confident of our people and our strategy. The assault commences in thirty-six hours. Operation Colonel Bogey is underway.'

The weather at the beginning of 'Colonel Bogey Day' gave no indication of the conflict to come. It was one of those wonderful summer mornings that guarantees hours of sunshine; clear blue skies, warm air, and just the slightest hint of a breeze. A perfect day for a round of golf. And perfect visibility for anybody about fifteen centimetres high scanning the course with a toy telescope, or for a flight of pigeons silently swooping in from the west and unloading their breakfast on unsuspecting players below. It was the first wave, striking the early psychological blow and also highlighting targets for the artillery if needed.

In a tent, camouflaged beneath some bushes, General Thorclan and his female assistant, Gniptip, were holding the day's first news conference. The reporters of all the important papers were there; the *Daily Provincial*, the *Cascadian Sport*, the *Reflector*, the *Elysian Intellect*, and of course the *Moon*.

'Ladies and Gentlemen, thank you for coming this morning. Inevitably there is a news blackout operating at present, but as soon as any details can safely be released, you will be the first to know. I *can* tell you that all our troops are safely entrenched in their various positions, and are watching for any MiGs.'

'MiGs, General?' asked the man from the *Reflector*.

The reporter from the *Elsyian Intellect* got there ahead of Thorclan. 'Military Golfers, you fool,' he whispered. 'What do you think they are, aeroplanes?'

'Any early action you can tell us about, General?' asked a young lady, Duripaxe, from the *Provincial*.

'A brief aerial bombardment from a squadron of wood pigeons, just a softening-up exercise.'

'Love it,' said Snoghod, the man from the *Moon*, with great relish. 'I can already see the headline – *SPLAT!*'

'You shouldn't need reminding,' added the cool and sharp voice of Gniptip, 'that we bear no ill-will towards these MiGs. Our action is *purely* defensive. They have trespassed beyond the legitimate frontier of the fairways – and some have even gone out of bounds. This campaign is about halting aggression, not stirring up hatred or causing unnecessary suffering. They may be golfers, but they are still human beings. 'Splat' is entirely inappropriate.'

'Don't worry, darling,' replied the *Moon* man. 'Easily sorted. What about *One in your eye, MiG!?*'

Kul, the Foreign Correspondent on the *Cascadian Sport*, raised a hand. 'General, will the new Assistant Guide be involved, as he is more their size? Also where will the Assembly's Inspection Team be based?'

'Good questions. The Team will be by the Clubhouse to assess the parting comments of the combatants. The Assistant Guide will be anywhere and everywhere, but not part of the actual conflict. This is purely a Grecian matter.' As he finished speaking there was a 'crack' in the distance. 'Right,' said Thorclan crisply, 'sounds like the first rounds are being shot. Meeting closed; keep an eye on my Leader Board during the day to see how the conflict is progressing.'

The General marched off, and Gniptip rapidly gathered up her papers, and the reporters wrote up their notes for the next editions.

Jamie had been asked by Thorclan not to interfere in the fighting. '*We've* got something to prove this time,' the General had stressed, 'like you had with Gratton. Just wander around the combat zones and enjoy the Grecian Army in action. And join us near the Clubhouse later; if the Inspection Team's happy, the next Provincial Assembly will be a formality.'

Jamie was seated on the steps of the Rotunda, the very centre of the war zone. He was enjoying the sunshine and the gentle

movement of players around the course, and it was hard to believe
that just off the fairways there was a military campaign being
waged. Occasionally he heard a cry from a golfer, or saw another
one practising his aim after firing a loose shot, but mostly it was
a scene of steady and quiet endeavour.

He looked through his binoculars. Nothing unusual anywhere.
He panned round, trying to spot tell-tale signs of MiGs. It wasn't
easy. They all looked the same; perhaps they were in disguise.

And then he saw them on the first tee. Two young men, in jeans
and trainers, one laughing out loud as his partner overstruck the
missile into the trees. 'That's them!' muttered Jamie to himself.
'Military Golfers!'

He was tempted to run on and warn the soldiers in Sector 4, but
he knew that was totally contrary to orders. He mustn't interfere.
All he could do was casually walk over and keep his head down.
He desperately hoped that the villains had been spotted.

The two of them lobbed a few missiles around the first zone, and
then showed their true cunning. As Jamie watched, he realised that
they were making a rapid advance, deliberately missing out Sectors
2 and 3. 'Good grief,' he gasped, 'a surprise attack!'

He broke into a run, and then dived into a small group of trees,
but the MiGs had been incredibly quick. They were in position for
their first shot in Sector 4. Jamie watched with his heart in his
mouth. Were Thorclan's troops ready?

He needn't have worried. As the first MiG was about to swing, a
squirrel walked across in front and stood about one metre in front
of the tee. It stared at the ball. The two golfers fell about laughing.
They tried to shoo it away. It refused to budge. They moved the
missile to the left. The squirrel moved to the left. They moved the
tee back. The squirrel matched the position. They were now getting
frustrated. 'For goodness' sake, just belt the thing!' shouted one, but
the animal quickly grabbed the ball and disappeared with it. 'Oi!
Come back you rat!' yelled the other.

His partner collapsed in hysterics. 'It's not a rat, it's a squirrel,
you idiot!' That didn't go down too well, and Jamie watched the
two of them start to push each other around. They were rolling around
on the ground when a senior Club Member came across and instructed

that for them the game was over.

'A first-rate victory,' thought Jamie, 'and a very brave squirrel. Looked like a 'L'-Class – still got some fight in it.'

Sector 8 was nearby, so Jamie sauntered over to the smooth green of the landing site, highlighted by a flag. This Sector had been identified as being particularly critical; the Cascadians had suffered heavy shelling here for years. They had even been shot at on the water.

He didn't have long to wait. A group of four players appeared, one of whom was clearly a danger to life and limb. He was lagging some way behind the rest, and his missile had plummeted into the desert area, a wide sandy valley. As Jamie watched, he noticed a Grecian soldier in light brown and cream combats, possibly Redah, creep forward through the sand with a small cone-shaped container and a spade. Quickly filling the bucket with sand, he emptied it carefully in front of the missile. And again . . . and again, until he had built a neat line of sandcastles. The final touch was a cone of sand perched delicately on top of the white sphere.

'Safely defused,' thought Jamie, 'very tidy job.'

When the foursome wandered over, one MiG didn't appreciate the fine workmanship involved, and blamed his companions, who found the whole thing hilarious. Strong words and one or two angry gestures were exchanged. Another victory for the Grecians.

Notable successes were being recorded elsewhere around the grounds. Jamie didn't see many for himself, but apparently Strenop's moment of glory came in Sector 9, when he fired an arrow from over three metres away and knocked out the tee precisely when a MiG was firing. The missile fell to the ground and rolled away backwards down the slope. This incredible accuracy and timing became a popular topic of conversation in many dining rooms, whether human or Grecian.

The contest for the most heroic action of the day was easily won by the team in Sector 7, where four highly-trained divers (wearing Action Man Moon Helmets) had hidden amongst the reeds at the lake's edge. They had emerged from cover swiftly and silently on several occasions, and by the end of the day had started up the engines of no less than nine golf trolleys (the dreaded motorised carriers). This had sent them careering off across the course, out of control and pursued by MiG owners. Rather wonderfully, four of the carriers had turned full circle and splashed into the water at full speed.

Two had been immediately followed by their distressed owners, performing a synchronised dive that would have graced the Olympics.

The result was a foregone conclusion. At the end of the conflict, Thorclan met with the Listener and three inspectors, one from each of the other provinces, and they were unanimous in their verdict. The day had been full of undesirable types who had left complaining about sharp objects in the long grass, weird animals, faulty equipment, lost balls, and strange smells. There had also been the oddest noises at the most inconvenient times, including a terrific sneeze by the launch-pad in Sector 6 just when a MiG was on his downswing. His partner had vehemently claimed that it had originated from the statue of George II high on a column behind them, which was obviously a complete lie and had therefore provoked a huge argument.

The Inspection Team rated the day as a glorious victory, and even though the proposal would still have to be passed in the Provincial Assembly, the Listener thought it would go through very smoothly. In their considered opinion, the Grecian Army had shown it was perfectly capable of defending all the borders.

Jamie was really excited. This could be the start of a period of progress amongst the provinces, and he knew that Granny would be absolutely thrilled. Her dreams of unity were starting to come true. He also felt that being this Assistant Guide was not proving to be too difficult.

Nevertheless, he was worried about one incident during the war.

During the afternoon, he had been making his way towards the old acacia tree that stood rather bare and forlorn in the centre of Sector 7. Yenech, the General's driver, had been positioned up in the tree all day, well hidden in a small hollow. He had done a superb job of signalling to the forces below, but had become too casual as the day had gone on. One of the final group of golfers had fired off a powerful wood shot that had cannoned into the tree, ricocheted off some branches, and had finally rolled down a wider bough and from behind knocked the little man off his perch. The drop to the ground, even into long grass, was massive for a person of his size.

Jamie was about fifty metres away and had seen it all.

Running as fast as he could, he was dismayed to see someone else get there ahead of him and pick up the fallen Grecian soldier.

Vicky. And she was inspecting it closely, lifting the arms up and down.

Before she had been able to ask any questions, an out of breath Jamie had persuaded her to hand over the small figure, claiming it was a toy that he had accidentally thrown up in the tree earlier that day. Vicky appeared not to have noticed anything unusual about it. Jamie, hoping she'd believed him, had walked off with Yenech in his pocket, and the little man had soon woken up, mainly thanks to the smelly old sweets stuck to him.

'What . . . what happened?' he muttered.

'You got hit in the rear by a missile,' explained Jamie, relieved that the little fellow had come to no harm. 'And then you fell out the tree.'

'Was that all?'

'And you got picked up by a sixteen year-old girl.'

'Seriously?' he said. And then added, rather glumly, 'And I thought I was dreaming. . . . I missed it all. . . . What did she look like? What did she say about me?'

'She was speechless,' said Jamie. 'And I don't think she's really your type.'

7: Vicky's Discovery

'This is the life,' thought Jamie, leaning against his pillow. 'The summer holidays, living at Malplaquet, breakfast in bed, and the family miles away.' He worked through the files on his laptop, finally found *Seriously Boring Stuff,* and began to type up his entry for the previous day.

> *Monday July 31ˢᵗ. Superb start to Malplaquet campaign today. Glorious victory against the MiGs. Thorclan overjoyed; no Grecian casualties and luckily no prisoners-of-war.*

'Ahem!'

Somebody was at the foot of the bed. Jamie swiftly clicked the mouse to reduce the page, peered over the top of the screen, and spotted the unexpected visitor.

'Nigriff!' Jamie sighed with relief. 'Don't creep up on me like that!'

'My enormous apologies, sir,' he replied quickly. 'In what way *would* you like me to creep up on you?'

'Not in *any* way, Nigriff; you made me jump. This is all top-secret stuff; nobody else must see it. I didn't know who you were.'

'Didn't know who I *was*, sir? I don't understand. I've *always* been me, and I believe that my personality has remained consistent over many moons. My ancestral line is remarkably pure. However, my *titles* are a recent addition, so a change. . . .'

'No, Nigriff, you don't understand. . . .'

'Quite right, sir, I don't understand. At least, I *do* understand that I *don't* understand,' answered the Imperial Archivist with a puzzled frown.

'How did we get into this mess?' thought Jamie, and then addressed his little friend. 'Nigriff, it's too early for this. Let's start again.' He took a deep breath. 'Good morning, Nigriff. What can I do for you?'

'Oh, nothing particular, sir, I just came to see how you were.'

'I *was* fine,' replied Jamie, and then corrected himself before the conversation got tangled up again. 'I mean, I *am* fine. Are you okay?'

'Not exactly, sir. I don't think I'm really, well, not *myself* this morning.'

Jamie hesitated. He decided not to ask Nigriff *who* he was this morning, but instead chose a subtle response to help things along. 'Really?'

'Indeed, sir. It's an odd feeling; a strange mixture of delight at the victory of the Grecians, but also some – how shall I put it? – *concern* at what may happen next.'

'Like the MiGs fighting back?'

'No, not at all. It's more to do with how things might *change* around here.'

'Well, all I can see is the provinces co-operating more. That's what Granny wants, isn't it?'

'Ye-es,' Nigriff replied hesitantly. 'That has always been *her* ambition. . . .'

Their conversation was interrupted by Granny talking loudly downstairs, much more loudly than usual. 'Yes, that's right, he's upstairs, the bedroom on the left. Jamie!' she shouted up. 'Surprise visitor for you!'

'Nigriff!' he hissed. 'Quick, under here!' He lifted the edge of the duvet and the Most Notable Librarian crawled under with a helpful shove from behind. Only a second later Vicky walked in.

'Morning, Jamie,' she said breezily. 'I just popped in to see how you were.'

'Oh, um, I *was* fine,' gulped Jamie, 'I mean I still am, or at least it depends what you mean, or who. . . . '

Vicky gave him an odd stare. 'Whatever. Let's get to the point; I know you're up to something, possibly something very weird. I'm not moving from here until you tell me what's going on.'

With that she plonked herself down on the edge of the bed, just where Nigriff lay hidden. Jamie held his breath; the Librarian was probably being slowly pulped. Any moment now, and the Murder section in the Imperial Archives would have a new entry. He didn't know what to say or do. So he just looked at Vicky.

'Nothing? Okay, let's recap. Talking to rabbits was odd, but I just took that as a typical adolescent male thing, y'know, trying to recapture your lost childhood, replacement teddy-bear, stuff like that. What made me *really* suspicious, was you saying that figure I found was a toy.'

'It was a toy – I'd been playing with it!'

'Maybe you had, but the point, Jamie Thompson – and I can't believe I'm saying this – is that the little soldier was alive.'

'No, it wasn't. It was unconscious, I mean . . . er, stiff.'

'*Stiff*?' she queried, raising her voice and leaning towards Jamie, who was mightily relieved to see a small hump creeping away from her. 'What do you mean, stiff? The legs and arms were *moving*, for goodness sake!'

'It's a new type,' said Jamie hurriedly, 'you know, realistic. Almost human.'

Vicky wasn't persuaded. 'It was breathing,' she added firmly.

'Microchips?' he replied, rather optimistically. 'They can do amazing stuff nowadays. The chest goes up and down and everything. Honest, it's a toy, really.'

'Jamie, you're being ridiculous,' Vicky said firmly, and positioned herself right in the centre of the bed. The moving hump came up against this new obstacle, stopped briefly and moved off across the bed. 'It wasn't a toy. It was a little man – warm, and *alive*.'

Jamie noticed Granny outside the door, unseen by Vicky. The old lady knew the game was up, and was nodding slowly, looking resigned. He took the hint.

'Vicky, there's something I need to tell you.'

'Really?' she said, in mock amazement.

'Well, you know that toy soldier you found yesterday. . . .' He then explained most of what he had discovered so far. It included the strange sighting of footprints at the picnic, meeting Nigriff, finding out about the four provinces, then Thorclan and the Grecian Army, and finally yesterday's war.

Vicky sat deep in thought. Since the shock of finding this living small soldier, she had done nothing but think about tiny people. Jamie's information certainly answered some of her questions about the little person, but not all of them.

'So what are they – leprechauns? They're not Borrowers, are they?'

Jamie heard a muffled cry of indignation from beneath the duvet, and loudly shuffled his feet to hide the noise.

'Er, I think Granny had better answer that question.' On cue, she padded into the room in her slippers.

Granny filled in a few of the gaps; how the people were actually descendants of Lilliputians, and had lived in a succession of places – the island in the Lake, the model city in the Japanese Gardens, and finally, after the Great Divergence, in four separate provinces.

Jamie was staggered at how calmly Vicky was taking it. 'Aren't you surprised?' he asked.

Vicky laughed. 'Surprised? Of course not . . . this sort of thing happens all the time.' And then, seeing Jamie's face, 'Only kidding. . . . Come on, it's ludicrous, completely whacky. Mind you, once I'd met your friend yesterday, I assumed he wasn't the only one. The *Gulliver's Travels* idea does make some sense.'

'But don't you find it odd that they're *here,* in Malplaquet?'

'Funnily enough, no. The gardens *are* special, they've got an atmosphere, I don't know what exactly. Tiny people living here seems to fit somehow.'

Jamie thought that he'd never understand the way girls' minds worked – perhaps it was this 'female intuition' he'd heard about. Then again, it might explain why Vicky had seen Yenech so easily; presumably she had this special 'feel' for the gardens that Granny talked about.

Nevertheless, Vicky was puzzled. 'How do they manage though? What about eating, keeping warm in the winter, clothes and things?'

Granny went over some details of the Lilliputians' lives, explaining that in the early days in the Japanese Gardens it had been easier. Their real problems had only started after the Great Divergence, when they moved out of their purpose-built accommodation.

'The obvious places to live in were the temples, which were in a wonderfully poor state, with plenty of cavities and hollow bits inside, lovely places for their homes. But now the National Trust is restoring them, they're not so good. So they've found lots of other places to hide in.'

'What about clothes?'

'Ever bought anything from the WI stall in town?' asked Granny, smiling.

'Only your dolls' outfits . . . oh, I see,' replied Vicky. 'All made by you?'

'Not all,' said Granny. 'Sometimes I've sold things the Lilliputians have made. They like to help pay for their upkeep – and their work is amazing.'

Jamie thought of something downstairs. 'Is that wedding-veil one of theirs?'

Granny nodded. 'A story for a rainy day, Jamie.'

'Do you get food for them as well?' asked Vicky.

'They manage quite well in the summer with fruits and grain, and they are fine hunters. They know which fish are particularly tasty – and where to get a decent slab of cake. Like all little people, I suppose.'

'I suppose it's a pain the school being here, isn't it?' said Vicky.

'Actually that's helped. There's always plenty of food to be found in the outlying storehouses – the kitchen staff blame rats –

and the school uses some of the temples for teaching rooms, so they're lovely and warm in winter. The Queen's Temple is perfect for a short break in February – you even get entertained by Mr. Harris' delightful clarinet pieces.'

Jamie imagined little families flicking through catalogues of winter holiday destinations, checking out the sizes of radiators, the number of heating vents, or whether the accommodation included live music.

Vicky was thinking fast. 'So do you want them all back together, like before?'

'No,' replied Granny, shaking her head, 'they'd be found too easily. It's best if they carry on living where they are, but they must *feel* they belong together, that they're not totally different. They think the Lilliput stories are just old myths. It's so sad. I'd love it if they knew about their real history, who they really are.'

'Okay, I get the idea. One last question – can I meet one that can talk to me?'

Jamie answered immediately – he was worrying about how much air there was under a duvet. 'How about right now?'

'Fine. There's actually one in this room?' she said, twisting round and looking over the edge of the bed.

'Er, yes,' replied Jamie, 'he's our undercover agent.' He pulled back the duvet to reveal Nigriff, curled up in a ball, desperately trying to remain out of sight. 'This one will definitely talk to you.'

Once they had unrolled Nigriff, and he had got over the shock of his discovery, matters proceeded very well. He was pleased to discover that Vicky had once worked in the local Library on Saturday mornings, and for her part, she was very intrigued by his extensive vocabulary and manner of speaking. She said it reminded her of some old books she had recently studied for GCSE English. Vicky also reassured them that the big secret was safe with her, and also that she might be able to help out at weekends when she was a Trust Volunteer. 'It'll be useful for me as well, because I want to do a Gap Year working with under-developed. . . .' She stopped, realising what she had just said.

Nigriff was looking most insulted, but Granny explained that 'under-developed' was not a reference to a person's size, but to

He pulled back the cover to reveal Nigriff

a society that was improving.

To finish their discussion on a proper note, and to formally confirm Vicky's role, they composed a brief document for her to sign. Jamie opened up a new file, (*More Boring Than You Could Possibly Imagine*), and Vicky typed the following:

I, Victoria, do solemnly swear on this day, the First of August, that I will

i.   Keep secret the existence of the people of Malplaquet
ii. Respect and protect their different customs and practices
iii. Watch where I am walking and sitting, especially on beds
iv. Uphold the good name of Librarians and Archivists
v.   Help to bring about a new Empire

Signed (typed) Vicky

Nigriff complimented her upon her language and perception, suggesting that point (iv) about Librarians was particularly well-expressed, and also that point (v) on the Empire was the subject of many of their old stories. 'We have great hopes of a better life. The young master has expressed his desire to help us achieve this.'

'Not forgetting the new defence force, Nigriff,' added Granny pointedly. 'If we all pull together, you never know what we can achieve.'

'This is great,' added Vicky. 'We might make this dream come true.'

'You might make Yenech's dreams come true,' thought Jamie.

Jamie had been reading about the history of Malplaquet and its gardens, knowing that his Father would ask about them. He had found that the owner of Malplaquet in the early days, one Sir Richard Temple, had amassed a substantial fortune, partly from the King as a reward for his courageous leadership in battle, but also from his marriage to the daughter of a rich brewer. He had spent his new wealth on some major extensions to his home, creating an impressive mansion.

He had also carried out major works on his estate, constructing a criss-cross of paths and walks in the gardens and parkland, all of them as straight as an arrow and ending in interesting monuments and buildings. The plans of those early gardens looked like intersecting spiders' webs and star shapes – very precise and geometrical, but perhaps rather dull to walk along.

Then, as Jamie read more, he discovered something odd. He had been looking at pictures of these early maps, and had noticed a dramatic and fundamental change over a very small period of time. All the *straight* lines disappeared; the paths instead became floppy; wandering around the grounds like lots of snakes. The hard edges of the lakes became gentle curves, and open glades in woodlands changed from being neat squares to all sorts of fluffy shapes, like clouds. The early plans looked like they had been plotted by a mathematician, the later ones drawn by an artist.

Jamie knew which ones he preferred, partly because that was how Malplaquet still looked. 'Much more natural,' he thought to himself.

He found he couldn't get the contrast in plans and designs out of his mind. They were so radically different in style.

He typed up a few notes, saved them in *Some Incredibly Interesting Holiday Work* and then sat looking at the words he had just written; 'These changes took place in the early eighteenth century'.

That was when the Lilliputians had first appeared at Malplaquet.

The quiet chatter of the PRs in the Gothic Temple was interrupted by the Listener's shrill voice.

'SILENCE !'

She stared round at the delegates as they respected her words of command and rapidly settled themselves around the circular rug. Jamie was still a fringe member – and by his side sat Vicky, watching the unfolding events with great interest. She was staggered at the number of tiny people who had been buzzing around the room.

'Quiet! The Assembly will begin.'

Vingal the Listener began proceedings by inviting one of the special inspectors at the Golf War, Goverghoil, to take centre-rug. On behalf of the Provincial Assembly, he stressed the enormous debt of gratitude that was owed to General Thorclan and his Army. He praised their wise tactics, careful use of weaponry, and their noble intention to enforce the MiGs' withdrawal rather than inflict injury. Then, as a token of the Assembly's gratitude, and as a sign of its confidence in their future defenders, he awarded Thorclan the title of 'Great Lord Of Battles' (GLOB), which seemed to embarrass the old commander. He was quite overcome by such a distinguished-sounding honour.

After the applause had died down, the Listener moved on to the other item on the agenda: the details of the 'Cold Stream Cup' Competition for that year.

'There shouldn't be any surprises,' she said vigorously, 'as you've known the date for a while. I trust all the provinces have been training. Four people per team.'

Jamie leaned down towards Nigriff. 'What's this all about?' he whispered.

'It's one of our Inter-Provincial Competitions, sir,' replied Nigriff. 'Actually it's not really a competition in the *strictest* sense of the word – more like a foregone conclusion. The Cascadians have won the Cup every year since the event started.'

'How come?'

'As ever,' continued the Listener's announcement, 'there are three parts to the contest; a run, a swim across the lake, and the final dash up the Cold Stream itself. In the dark.'

'Don't bother, Nigriff, I've just worked out why,' added Jamie. 'That lot sound like Cascadian specialities.'

'Any other business?' snapped Vingal.

'Yes, if I may,' broke in one PR (Thrayshal, Palladian). 'Who's the human with the new Assistant Guide?'

Almost as one, the members of the Assembly turned to face Vicky. They gasped, as if seeing her for the first time. Vicky herself blushed profusely.

'Noble PRs,' said Jamie humbly, hoping to reassure them, 'I can explain her presence.'

'*Presents*?' exclaimed an older Representative, looking excited. 'She's brought presents? That's alright then. She can come again.'

'You should know,' continued Jamie, 'that I have told my very good and trusted friend Vicky about your presence in the gardens.'

'*Our* presents?' said the same man, getting agitated. 'In the gardens? *I* haven't got any! Have other people got some? Did we vote on it?'

The Listener was looking sternly at Jamie, and at Nigriff, fidgeting nervously. 'Young sir, your record so far shows that we should trust *you*. But this spreading of knowledge about us to more humans seems excessive. Do explain.'

'It's very simple. She'll be helping me with the security and happiness of the four provinces, and, um, I've got a suggestion about that.'

Vicky was alarmed, wondering what Jamie was going to volunteer her for.

'In fact, I have *three* suggestions.'

Now Vicky was almost petrified.

'You'll need to vote about it of course, but these are my ideas. First, our better security now means the Cold Stream Cup could take place in daylight. [Some nods of approval] Second, there could be four extra sections, devised by the separate provinces. [A few grunts of disapproval, all of them Cascadian] Third, that I myself have a team. The "Thompson Quad Squad" will have a person from *each* province – two of my choosing, and two picked by you. I'd like to be involved in this famous contest.'

There was a massive hubbub of noise. Nigriff looked at him with wide-open eyes, wondering what on earth he was up to. Vicky was bemused and relieved at the same time.

The Listener brought the Assembly to order. 'Right,' she declared, 'you've heard the proposals. We'll take them as one lot, as they were all outlined in one speech. Those in favour?'

Three-quarters of the delegates made circles around their eyes.

'Those against?'

The Cascadians held their noses.

'The Eyes have it. Motion carried!'

As Jamie and Vicky walked out, with Nigriff being bounced along in his top pocket, she asked Jamie why he was entering a team like that. A mixed one was a good idea, but surely they wouldn't stand a chance against the Cascadians?

'It'll be a different competition, much fairer with the new parts. Remember the second proposal?' said Jamie.

'Well, I only hope you know what you're doing.'

'I think so. Anyway, let's hope Nigriff knows what *he's* doing.'

'What do you mean?'

'I doubt he's been in the Cold Stream Cup before.'

They both heard a small cry of dismay, and Jamie felt next to his shirt, a tiny figure collapse, presumably in a faint.

'We'd better start the training as soon as we can,' he added. 'Another big job. Could be more difficult than defeating Gratton.'

8: The Cold Stream Cup

'Nigriff, why can't you get excited about the Thompson Quad Squad?' Jamie was frustrated with Nigriff's continuing disinterest in the Cold Stream Cup.

'To be honest, sir,' he answered glumly, 'there is simply no point. As I have already said on eight occasions, the outright winner is certain.'

'Rubbish,' retorted Jamie, 'you can never tell, especially with the new competition. You can't give up before we start!'

'Sir, it's much easier to give up *before*, rather than *after*. It's going to be one long drawn-out process of embarrassment for all of us – especially for me.'

'It won't be that bad. A couple of the events might be tricky, but the new Elysian section is bound to suit you.' He explained that Nigriff's friends had proposed a number of ideas, including four-a-side Chess (with a 'Golden Check' rule if scores were level after extra-time), or the fastest summary of Plato's philosophy, but they had happily accepted the committee's final decision. The suggestions from the Palladians and Grecians might even help them. 'The point is, Nigriff, that our team consists of one person from each province, so we're in the strongest position. We've got one person who's really good at each test.'

'Of course, sir . . . and three who are really useless. Do

consider the team. Apart from the undeniably limited talents displayed by yours truly, we have Yenech – not our world's greatest soldier – and what about the two others foisted on you? Hyroc is a pleasant and big fellow, but the worst Cascadian swimmer for generations, and then there's Wesel.'

Jamie said nothing. He had been chatting with Granny last night, and she had specifically said that any of the Palladians would be fine, apart from Wesel. 'A lovely chap, but Palladians generally have a wide range of practical skills. He has one.' That talent turned out to be erecting temporary buildings – astonishingly temporary if it drizzled or there was a slight breeze. 'He calls it 'architectural recycling' but most others call it shoddy workmanship.'

So that was the TQS team; Nigriff, all brain and one run to his credit, Yenech, poor soldier and no better driver, and Hyroc and Wesel, an embarrassment to their own provinces. Things weren't looking good.

Two days later and they still weren't looking good. To tell the truth, they were now looking desperate.

The four members of TQS had been unhappy about merely standing near each other, let alone trying to co-operate, so the actual training was a dismal failure. Jamie had rapidly thrown together an obstacle course of logs and random lumps of wood, but it had simply fascinated Wesel, who kept on stopping to admire what he regarded as fine examples of his own craft. Hyroc the Cascadian hated being up to his neck in water in an old paddling-pool, and they had all loathed squelching around in the muddy corner of a field. 'You've got to get used to it,' Jamie had yelled. 'The Cold Stream at the end might decide whether we win or not.'

'It might decide whether I *live* or not,' Nigriff had muttered.

It was the night before the competition, and they were sat on the sofa at Granny's, feeling decidedly sorry for themselves. The old lady swept into the room, beaming broadly and carrying a large box.

'Right, just finished. Enough moping, it's time for a bit of self-respect. Jamie, hand these round. I'm not having my boys going out badly-dressed.'

The kit was wonderful. The green parade uniforms for the Drill section were immaculate, with hard-edged creases on the trousers and the shirts starched flat, and the boots must have been through a polishing-machine. Best of all was the gear for the major part of the competition; red running shorts, and blue and white vests that were quartered across the front, emblazoned with the bold yellow letters, 'TQS.'

'Wicked!' breathed Jamie, almost in awe. The four team-members gingerly held them as if they were holy objects. 'This is more like it,' said Yenech with quiet enthusiasm. 'I've never had a uniform this smart. Can we keep it afterwards?'

'Oh, I don't know really,' said Granny thoughtfully, 'but it would be only fair to let the *winners* keep them, don't you think?'

Nigriff, showing unusual interest in the military outfit, cleared his throat and spoke up. 'Madam, on behalf of us all, can I say how much we appreciate the efforts you have made to equip us? You clearly have great confidence in us, and therefore we should have far more confidence in ourselves. We *will* give of our best tomorrow. We will not let you or the young Master down. TQS – the Cold Stream Cup awaits!' His three team-mates responded by punching the air with their fists and shaking hands.

Jamie was delighted by their reactions, although under no illusions. Winning the Cup demanded much more than turning up well-dressed. But at least their attitude was right, and who could tell what might happen on the day?

As the sun rose on that clear August morning, gently warming into life the lakes and gardens, it picked out by Granny's house a gathering of about twenty small people, most of them dressed impeccably in lightweight green army outfits. They were checking each other's kit; dusting specks off shoulders, adjusting berets to the correct angle, tightening belts, and trying to avoid stepping on the boots of their *own* team. Leaders were giving final instructions.

'Remember last year's mistakes.'

'It's *seven* different sections this time . . . pace yourselves.'

'Think of the dinner tonight.'

'The Cascadians are definitely sunk this time.'

Vicky was standing by the other Lake Pavilion, keeping an eye open for any early-morning walkers, joggers, or cyclists, and she had a loud and rasping duck whistle as a warning if necessary. As it was only 5.45 am, she was expecting few problems – apart from keeping herself awake.

General Thorclan was the final arbiter as usual. His sense of fairness was legendary – as shown by the unbroken sequence of Cascadian success. The winning team in each section would gain five points, the second four etc, down to the worst, acquiring only one point. The scores after the six parts would determine the starting-positions for the muddy charge up the Cold Stream. There was a further five points for this race, and the highest total at the end would win the Cup.

The moment arrived. Granny called the first team forward. 'Grecians on the Parade Ground, please!'

Even when merely walking these soldiers appeared well-drilled. They approached the Lake Pavilion, confidently strode up the plank sloped above the steps, and took up their positions in two rows on the open flagstone floor. Their army chaplain, Rev. Nilleoc, barked out the first command. 'Grecian Drill Squad, Squad shun!' Heels clicked and bodies tightened as one. 'Move to the left in file, left TURN!' They turned through ninety degrees, as smoothly as a door on its hinges. 'By the right, quick MARCH!' Their self-assurance and smooth rhythm were both stunning.

'I think we'll go for second place here,' whispered Yenech to Wesel after the superb display. 'We can't beat that. It was faultless.'

'We won't be last anyway,' replied Wesel, 'a Cascadian's just marched off the edge.'

The sudden absence of Yargg the Cascadian threw that team into complete confusion. They weren't sure whether to ignore him, peer over to see if he had landed safely, or re-form in a line of three. They chose the last option, which really confused the missing comrade when he clambered back up the steps. Yargg tagged on to the end of the line, and then found himself being marched over the drop on the other side.

Other teams performed much better, although inevitably none as well as the Grecians. The Quad Squad reckoned they only got a couple of points (Hyroc had stuffed his hands in his pockets when told to stand at ease). First and last places were easily allocated, and the teams moved off towards the nearest undergrowth, which concealed the Assault Course that Granny and Vicky had constructed.

Points so far: Grecians: 5; Elysians: 4; Palladians: 3; TQS: 2; Cascadians: 1.

'Not a bad start, at least we didn't come last,' said Hyroc as they got changed into the special athletics kit. 'It's great the Cascadians are bottom for a change.'

Nigriff was his usual cautious self. 'As they apparently say in our Master's world, Mr. Hyroc, 'the game's not over yet'. There is a stern test ahead.'

In front was the Assault Course. The teams had to run along planks that were suspended at their shoulder height, crawl under a large brown cloth spread out just above the ground, squeeze through an old drainpipe with a nasty double 'S' bend, negotiate a rope walkway slung between two trees, and finally get over a solid and high wooden wall before a sprint to the line.

The Cascadians, trying to make up for their poor start, were surprisingly good at this. One of them was impervious to pain, throwing himself along the course with a total disregard for safety. 'That's one of the Zechsan brothers,' muttered Hyroc. 'The man's got no fear – he'd run through a wall just for fun.' Which was precisely what he was doing. After inflicting some damage on himself and the offending object, he decided to go over rather than through it, and sat astride the top, helping his mates to scramble up. The time was good; 2 minutes, 14 seconds.

The Elysians were not the fittest squad, but with their massive brainpower they analysed their tactics and teamwork, and emerged just 8 seconds behind the Cascadians. The Grecians, loving this physical challenge, ended with an unsurprising 2 minutes, 9 seconds. Jamie was happy finishing just ahead of the Elysians (mainly thanks to Hyroc dragging and shoving Nigriff through the pipe at great speed).

'Only the Palladians to come on this,' he thought to himself, 'and we really need the three points. The Grecians are running away with it.'

His luck was in. The Palladians were unimpressed with the standard of workmanship of the obstacles, inspecting each as if it was entered for an Arts and Crafts Exhibition. The wall was their biggest disappointment. One of them whistled to himself as he fingered the wood, splintered by Zechsan's misguided enthusiasm.

'Here, Chillkin, what d'you reckon to this?' He beckoned to his team-mate.

'Dear me. Worse than we thought.' He twisted off a plank.

'Thought so,' continued the first. 'See that? Rotten; you're looking at, well, wouldn't like to say exactly. Best to have a complete re-fit – save money in the long run. Tell you what, I'll do you a special deal. I've got a mate. . . .'

The Palladians gained one point, leaving them last after two sections.

Points so far: Grecians: 10; Elysians: 6; TQS: 5; Cascadians: 5; Palladians: 4.

The Assault Course result determined the starting places on a drain cover below the boundary wall, the traditional beginning of the Long Run. General Thorclan approached Vicky as she was leaning over, watching the runners manoeuvre into position. 'My dear, it's impossible at my age – and my height – to see exactly what's going on down there. Could you provide a running commentary?'

'I'm not sure about 'running,' General; I'd overtake them. How about a walker's?'

'Splendid – much better idea.'

Vicky put her clenched fist near her mouth, like a commentator speaking into a microphone, and her voice took on a strained, high-pitched whine. 'A few seconds before the start of the Malplaquet Grand Prize. The racers are on the grid, four Grecians by the pole. One whistle, two, three whistles, go, go, GO!' And she set off along the stone edging, keeping a close eye on events below.

'Heading past the copse, Sevegar the Grecian is leading, one of TQS on his heels, could be Yenech – yes it is, already moved up *six* places from the grid! *Superb* little runner! Now past some buckets, round the curve with a view of the Chapel, a lot of bunching, and . . . oh, my word! Senoj the Palladian has clipped an Elysian, swerved off into that old tyre . . . trying to rejoin, sliding on a patch of gravel . . . he's back on track! Amazing – kept running all the time!'

Thorclan was way behind, so Jamie placed him in his top pocket for a grandstand view. Granny was just enjoying the early-morning air, not bothered about following the race too closely. Vicky was still keeping up her walker's commentary.

'At the end of the straight, the runners shift down a gear into Stowe, the blue and white of TQS behind Sevegar, and . . . there's *another* casualty! Might be a Grecian . . . yes, it's Raida, lost a shoe, can't carry on, such bad luck! Questions about the constructors though – shoes shouldn't come off like that.'

As the leading runners careered around behind the Temple of Venus, only a few metres from the finish Yenech saw his chance.

'Sevegar's drifted too wide, he's left room on the inside, Yenech has seen it, he's put his foot down hard . . . there's not enough space, Sevegar's come across – oh my word, hit the stonework! Absolutely *lost* it! Sevegar was trying to run him off, smacked into the wall himself, the others are streaking past, and Yenech is going to take the five points for TQS! *What* a race!'

Jamie was delighted. He had been concerned that Yenech might get lost, but sensibly he had simply followed the wall. The TQS team celebrated and cooled down by splashing themselves with water (Nigriff being careful not to spoil his new running vest), and assessed their current ranking. 'By my reckoning,' gasped Yenech, 'we're second just behind the Grecians. They only got two points, so they're on 12 and we're on 10. We're beating the Cascadians, and the Palladians and the Elysians have only got 7 – this new Cup doesn't suit them.'

'Am I right in thinking, sir,' queried Nigriff, with an air of feigned innocence, 'that the *intellectual* challenge is next on the agenda?'

'Absolutely, Nigriff,' replied Jamie. 'Your moment of glory.'

The teams entered a small room at the back of Venus. On the floor lay five flat and square puzzles, with interlocking tiles that had to be slid around to form a picture of a boat. The Elysians rubbed their hands in glee, and dashed forward on the whistle. Their speed on the board was astonishing, and they claimed the five points within one minute. TQS were not far behind, once Nigriff had persuaded the others to stand back. The Cascadians were fine until one player jammed his fingers between two tiles, the Palladians made the mistake of lifting the pieces out to solve the problem, and the Grecians decided that the disorganised picture was a valuable piece of Modern Art (Post-Cubism) and should not be touched.

TQS had now leapt into the lead with 14 points, the Grecians were on 13, and the Cascadians were not yet out of it with 12 – and their traditional Cup specialities still to come. Equal third, thanks to that last victory (and much to their surprise), was the Elysian team. Nigriff was chatting happily with them, giving encouragement for the challenges ahead. They were going to need it.

The Palladians, lagging slightly behind on 9, improved on the Structural Section, their own proposal. A collection of old toy building blocks – cubes, columns, and prisms – had to be quickly formed into a solid and attractive edifice. No problem for the professionals, whistling as they worked, who constructed something that would have graced a Theme Park entrance. That put them up to 14 points. The Elysians had less success, building a completely solid shape that was logically perfect and totally impractical – no windows or doors etc. Wesel did a good job bearing in mind his reputation, producing a creation that broke almost all laws of physics, architecture, and good taste. It also fell down when the whistle blew. 'It's the echo in here,' he explained, 'it's far too strong.' TQS still gained 3 points, but the Grecians achieved second place and 4 points with an excellent castle.

Points so far: Grecians: 17; TQS: 17; Cascadians: 14; Palladians: 14; Elysians: 13.

The penultimate test was the famous Water-Crossing, requiring the teams to swim across a stretch of water, pushing a sizeable log (15 cms of broom handle) before them. The aquatic specialists took the five points, just in front of the Grecians, making a strong surge at the end. The Elysians gained yet another fifth place and one point. TQS managed a creditable third, to leave them one point below the Grecians, and thus to start half a metre behind them on the final event, the Cold Stream itself.

Points so far: Grecians: 21; TQS: 20; Cascadians: 19; Palladians: 16; Elysians: 14.

'It's a pity we're not in front,' said Jamie regretfully. 'Still, brilliant teamwork so far – but it's sheer guts now. Yenech, remember; the first to the Rotunda gets the five points.' They needed him to win – and a Grecian not to come second.

The teams of four were placed in their respective places at the start. Ahead lay the forbidding sight of the Valley of the Cold Stream. It was thirty metres long, bounded by steep sides, and boggy and treacherous throughout. At its far end lay a pipe disgorging a continuous flow of water down the ravine. Roughly half-way along, the stream was virtually blocked by a solid mass of earth and stones, built to provide a crossing-point for Golfers, but a narrow tunnel allowed the water (and small mammals) to pass through. Jamie whispered some final words of encouragement to Yenech, weary after his previous run. 'You know what to do; through the tunnel, get to the far pipe, climb out and sprint for the Rotunda. You can do it!'

The runners took up their positions on their starting-pebbles. A brief pause, the whistle blew, and Yenech took off like a man possessed, gaining rapidly on his rival Sevegar and actually overtaking him. 'Go Yenech!' screamed Jamie . . . and in utter disbelief watched his champion suddenly take a sharp left and disappear up a small pipe half-hidden in the bank. 'No, not that one, Yenech! Further on!' Jamie quickly slid half-way down the grassy slope towards the tube's dark opening. His frustrated cries rang down it. 'YENECH! Where are you?'

'Funny,' said a grinning Grecian, 'you could be his commanding officer.'

Jamie was devastated. None of his other three could win. He looked upstream; the other contestants were pressing on, oozing through knee-deep mud, slipping over on smooth stones, and sliding into each other. A few were already at the half-way tunnel, trying to squeeze into the entrance before the next man. As he watched, a blockage developed as the desperate bodies squashed together, and more runners further added to the chaos as they piled in from behind. Soon it was a Lilliputian log-jam. There was no way through.

Jamie squelched past the tunnel to see who might eventually emerge first, and glanced up to the far end of the valley – where he spotted Yenech clambering out of the main pipe, confused and dripping wet.

'YENECH!' he screamed. 'The Rotunda! Up the bank! GO FOR IT!'

The faithful driver waved and scrambled up the bank. Once on level ground, he looked back to the tunnel where a few muddy bodies were emerging on hands and knees, and then cheerily he jogged the short distance to the Rotunda. As he hauled himself over the final step, he was greeted by a rousing cheer from dozens of tiny people around the inside of the dome, and a warm handshake from Thorclan. He was also given a kiss from the Listener, and blown one by Vicky – a wonderful welcome.

Sevegar, in spite of his earlier crash, actually did come in second for the Grecians. This meant that the final totals were as follows.

Grecians: 25; TQS: 25; Cascadians: 22; Palladians: 17; Elysians: 16.

It was a dead-heat. General Thorclan, however, showing his famous generosity of spirit and sense of fair play, ruled that as they had won the Cold Stream race itself, the outright winners of the Cup were . . . the Thompson Quad Squad!

Jamie couldn't have been more happy. Granny was absolutely ecstatic, and Nigriff himself was very proud of what he had achieved. The celebrations lasted for hours, and every province agreed that it had been the best competition ever.

None of these people would have been so joyful, however, if

they had known that the final victory scenes in the Rotunda had been watched through powerful binoculars, by a man in a dark grubby coat. He had been hiding in a small clump of trees, a large red book by his side. After making a few notes, he had slunk away out of sight.

Nobody had seen him. But he had seen everything; everything that he had wanted to see. Lots and lots of little people.

9: The Ancient Prophecy

Early the following morning Granny was surprised by a series of light knocks on her kitchen window. She opened it for her visitor.

'Morning, Nigriff. It's not often you're up with the dawn chorus.'

'No, Madam, you're quite right – and a good morning to you.'

'Not too early for a cup of hot chocolate?'

'Thank you, that would be most welcome; the dew has inflicted a bad case of rising damp. A warm drink might help to dry me out. I must confess as well that I slept fitfully last night – insomnia, I believe. I do need waking up.'

'Well, is it any wonder?' said Granny, half-seriously. 'I didn't say anything at the dinner, but *some* people were knocking back far too much *Chateau Bourbon*.'

'Madam, let me assure you that my sleeplessness did not result from over-indulgence. I enjoyed a small cup – or two – but I had insomnia for an entirely different reason.'

'Which was?'

'It was because I couldn't sleep.'

Granny thought about asking him *why* he couldn't sleep, but knew the answer would be, 'insomnia.' This was frustrating but also intriguing, because these circular conversations usually meant that Nigriff had something to say but couldn't come directly out with it. What was bothering him? She flicked the switch on the kettle and carried on chatting.

'Anyway, I was most impressed with your efforts yesterday. Who would have thought that *you* would be in the winning team – especially one composed of different provincials? And I must compliment you on your outfit. That combat jacket does suit you.'

'Er, yes . . . it just happened to be near my bed this morning,' replied Nigriff in some embarrassment. 'It is practical though – very good for hiding in, matches the undergrowth beautifully. My Elysian tailor might run up a spare one for me.'

'Well, I know Jamie was very proud of you all. Come to think of it, did you see him on your way here? He was up an hour ago; said he wanted a short walk.'

'No, Madam, I'm afraid I didn't. But we do need to talk with him when he returns. There are some absolutely essential matters to discuss.'

Granny looked straight at Nigriff and paused, realising that this was why he had come to see her. She said quietly, 'You think it's time, don't you?'

Nigriff nodded slowly. 'He has now proved himself, and it would not be fair to continue to keep him in the dark. It might even be dangerous to *all* of us to do so.'

'Nigriff, you're being dramatic again. But you're right; I'll get the box out. There's no chance of being disturbed at this time of day.'

Jamie was anxiously pacing up and down in front of the Pebble Alcove. After the previous day's events, he shouldn't have been worried. Winning the Cup with a *mixed* team had been a breakthrough, both for his role as a Guide and for his plans for the people.

But the strange images conjured up in the Alcove were bothering him. He didn't know *how* they appeared and so far they had been harmless, but could nasty things appear as well? If he had another go at it, would he see Gulliver again – or something else? He was apprehensive, but he wasn't going to get any answers by hanging around outside.

He took a deep breath, walked in and sat down on the semi-circular bench. Looking casually around the inside, he noticed the inlaid outline of a cow and stared at it. Just as before, trails of mist appeared across the entrance and grew denser, with images materialising on the screen. Jamie sat there, as if in a trance.

Under a stunning blue sky lay a wide expanse of beautiful and tranquil countryside. There were well-kept fields, tidy hedges, patches of woodland, peaceful lakes glinting through trees, and sheep and cows munching grass. Jamie felt very content, incredibly relaxed, almost physically lighter. The air smelled fresh, with a clean taste; he drew in great mouthfuls, trying to spread it down through his body. It was a wonderful sensation.

'It . . . it's beautiful,' he whispered, 'just like Malplaquet.' Then without warning the mist began to separate, and through the wisps he found himself staring at a very similar scene. 'This is stupid,' he thought crossly. 'It *is* Malplaquet. It's just showing this place.' He began to wonder if it was working properly. He quickly looked up at the mermaid, hoping to find himself back on the beach. Nothing happened. He anxiously scanned round all sorts of other outlines – a star, some flowers, a crescent moon, a bird of some sort. It was no good; none of them produced anything. The place seemed empty and cold, no longer mysterious – just a stone shelter with some odd patterns in it.

Jamie slipped off the seat, stuffed his hands in his pockets, and wandered off, briefly glancing back at the silent Alcove. He shrugged his shoulders and walked on, thinking of breakfast.

Both Nigriff and Granny heard the gate click shut.

'Who's going to start off?' asked Granny, looking pointedly at Nigriff standing in the centre of the table. Behind him was an antique box, about twice his height, russet-coloured, with a rounded top and a single clasp lock. At his feet lay a piece of yellowish paper, folded-up and tied across the centre with a red ribbon. It had the crumbly remains of sealing wax on it.

'Madam, as you have known him a great deal longer than I have, I do think that it falls to you to introduce the topic. Of course,' he added, patting the document, 'I shall enlarge upon this archive material. That is more *my* speciality.'

Jamie came in, and was pleased to see the small man.

'Hello, Nigriff, you're early. Couldn't sleep?'

'Well, as a matter of fact, I suffered from a touch. . . .'

'He's fine, Jamie,' interrupted Granny, 'still excited after yesterday.'

'Yesterday *was* brilliant,' added Jamie. 'Hey . . . nice jacket! Really suits you.'

'Thank you, sir, it does have its uses. My Elysian tailor. . . .'

'So what's that old piece of paper?' asked Jamie, spotting the item by Nigriff, and adding, with a smile, 'Your application for the Grecian Army?'

It was meant as a joke, but Nigriff didn't find it funny. He drew himself up to his full height, and prepared to make his feelings known. Again Granny intervened before the situation got out of control.

'Jamie, sit down a minute, we need to chat. All three of us.'

She pulled out a couple of chairs, and the two of them sat down. Jamie looked quizzically at her, and then at Nigriff – who had taken off his combat jacket.

'That paper's nothing to do with the Grecians, nor even Nigriff really. In fact for ages we weren't sure who the writing was all about. But we are now.'

She paused.

'It's *you*. We're certain of it.'

Jamie didn't know how to react. On the one hand, he was excited. The paper was obviously very old. It might involve a lot of money – maybe he was the new owner of some wonderful property. On the other hand, Granny was sounding serious, almost solemn, so it might be nothing to do with a fortune. It might even be bad news.

'Jamie, we both think you're very special – and very lucky.'

Well, that's a bit of a relief, thought Jamie. It can't be bad then.

Granny motioned to the little Archivist. 'Can you open up the poem, Nigriff?'

A *poem*? Jamie couldn't help feeling disappointed. It would have been far better if she had said, 'I think we need to open up the will, Nigriff.' And whoever heard of a poem being lucky – or anything to do with money?

Nigriff was struggling with the ribbon. 'I must admit that I haven't looked at this for a long time, Madam, and my fingers aren't what they used to be.' Then he stopped fiddling with the knot; a loop was tied tightly around one leg. 'I appear to have been captured and I am losing some feeling in that limb. The problem looks like a granny knot,' he added, 'and I would be very grateful if a granny could deal with it.' Which she duly did.

Soon the paper was lying unfolded on the table. It was very fragile, faded around the edges, and even torn along a couple of folds. Jamie leaned over to get a closer look. He could see faint brown handwriting, in a loose and flowing style.

Granny gently pressed it flat, and turned it slightly for Jamie to read more easily. 'This is a remarkable document,' she explained, 'remarkable for a number of reasons. Until this moment, Nigriff and I were the only people who were aware of its existence. Now there are three of us.' She hesitated to let this piece of information sink in. Jamie just stared at the paper. 'It was written in the early eighteenth century.'

Jamie now thought of money again; presumably this ancient manuscript was now his, and maybe he could auction it for hundreds (thousands?) of pounds. He could see a trip to Florida coming up. He also noticed the same period of history cropping up again.

'Nigriff, can you carry on?' asked Granny. 'This is much more your field; names and dates confuse me.'

'Thank you, Madam. I should be delighted.' He adjusted his collar, brushed the front of his shirt, and stood up even straighter than normal.

'Master Jamie, could I ask if you have ever heard of the poems of Pope?'

Jamie, wanting to appear intelligent, said he'd heard of the Catholic one, and he thought he lived in Rome, but he didn't know if he was a poet.

Nigriff seemed surprised, so Jamie knew he'd impressed him.

Soon the paper was lying unfolded on the table.

'Ah, ye-es, I see what you mean . . . although I wasn't thinking of
a Pope, but rather of the poet Pope himself – Alexander, from
your 1700s.'

Jamie now admitted his ignorance to Nigriff; he knew nothing
about popes in that century who wrote poetry. Nigriff sighed.
'No, young sir, this concerns a man called Pope – *name*, not
title. This is one of his poems. This is his actual handwriting,
and this,' he added with a flourish, pointing to the bottom of the
page, 'is his signature.'

Jamie peered at it respectfully, and could just make out the
name. 'Are you *sure*?' he asked, with sudden interest. He knew
autographs were worthless unless they were genuine.

'There is no doubt,' replied Nigriff, slightly irritated, as if his
professional expertise was being questioned. 'No doubt at all.'

'So what's it about?' asked Jamie.

'Alexander Pope was a man of many talents – not just a poet,
but also a traveller, and a cultured gentleman with a profound
appreciation of architecture and gardens. He wrote much in
honour of the first Duke of Malplaquet, praising his patriotism
and courage as well as his beautiful gardens. This is one such
piece.'

This was beginning to feel like school. 'Nigriff, I know you
like this stuff, but it's the summer holidays, and I did loads of
this sort of thing last term.'

'Master Jamie, do bear with me. It is important you understand
the writing's immediate, and I should say, *superficial* background.
I will now read it. Please concentrate, and notice the references
to the Duke and his virtues.'

As Nigriff prepared himself for the oration, Granny shuffled
over to the open door and, satisfied there was no-one around,
shut it tight. Nigriff stood level with the top line and, walking
down the page as he read, recited the verse.

'A Child no more, the Man appears,
He comes of Age, the Hope of Years.
Our Fount of Wisdom, whose Way is Delight,
True Source of all Pure Knowledge and Insight,

Our Guide, for whom the Bells do Ring,
Thy Presence much Warmth in Friendship Bring.
Thou makest the Sea-people great Appear,
This Blessed Island shalt have no Fear.
In every Quarter defend our Shores,
Unite our People, grow strong in Wars.
The Capital gained, our Frontiers Sealed,
Temples Restored, the Nation Healed.
Through thee the Great Empire newly Starts,
The Garden Kingdom, true Home of our Hearts.'

At the end he paused, sniffed slightly, and wiped his eyes with a dab of his pocket-handkerchief. He waited for Jamie's response.

'Er, that's, um, clever. Neat,' muttered Jamie, wishing he had paid more attention to his English teachers last year.

'It is a *remarkable* piece of writing,' stressed Nigriff, 'a worthy tribute to a great man. But the two of us both believe that it is not *just* in praise of a fine nobleman. Madam,' he added gravely, turning towards the lady in question, 'would you care to present our conclusions?'

She nodded. 'Jamie, we think it's prophetic.'

Unfortunately, Jamie didn't catch *precisely* what she had said. 'I wouldn't say it's that pathetic, Granny. I got most of it, especially the fighting and things. It's better than most poetry.'

Granny and Nigriff looked at each other. Nigriff counted to ten under his breath. She continued her explanation. 'No, Jamie, not *path*etic, but *proph*etic, like a prophecy – looking into the future, saying what you think is going to happen.'

'So is the first Duke going to do all that?' Jamie looked bemused. 'He's dead, isn't he?'

'Yes, of course, but it's not just about him. We think that Pope was really writing about some *other* person, in the future, who would come and do great things. Can you see? The poem looks like his usual writings about the Duke, but it's also about someone else. And we believe this person *has* now come.' She hesitated.

'As I said just now, Jamie. It's you.'

The first phrase that leapt into Jamie's mind was 'off her trolley,' closely followed by 'losing her marbles.' The trouble was that she was clearly serious, and so was Nigriff, and they didn't look as if they had suddenly gone crazy.

'Hang on a minute – how can it be me? I'm only thirteen – I can't run the country and fight wars and stuff like that!'

'But Jamie, that's exactly what you *have* been doing over the last few weeks. Not in England, but in *Malplaquet*. Do you see? Pope was describing the great leader that the people of Malplaquet need.'

'But why do you think it's me?'

'Look at the poem. Pope left some clues about the one he calls the Guide. Nigriff, can you run over the first lines?'

'Run, Madam?'

'I mean just read them, Nigriff.'

He walked back to the top of the page. 'Master Jamie, our belief is that the great leader of Malplaquet is described in these first seven lines. He is given glorious titles.' He pointed as he read down. 'Fount of Wisdom. . . . True Source of all Pure Knowledge and Insight.'

Jamie burst out laughing. 'Not what my teachers think,' he sniggered. 'My last reports didn't exactly say, *Jamie has been a true source of all pure knowledge and insight this term.*'

'Prophecy is mysterious in its nature, young sir, and this quality may not yet be obviously present. But there are also the Three Tests.'

Jamie looked concerned. 'The Three Tests? Is this something I've got to do?' He'd once read about what young people in primitive tribes did to prove their manhood – like walking over hot coals, drinking vast amounts of intoxicating liquids, or piercing sensitive parts of their anatomy.

Nigriff reassured him. 'Certainly not, sir. You have already taken them and, you will be pleased to know, passed with flying colours.' Then they explained to Jamie how he perfectly fitted the opening lines.

Firstly, the prophecy specifically referred to somebody 'coming of age.' On the exact day that he had become thirteen years old, when some think that boys become adults, he alone at the picnic had heard the bell: *Our Guide, for whom the Bells do Ring.*

'Hang on a minute,' said Jamie, 'what was that bell?'

'The old one on the gate round the corner,' answered Granny. 'The Lilliputians ring it as a warning before any fireworks start. They hate the tremors and noises.'

The second clue was when he had felt a sudden burst of heat whilst sat by the Temple of Friendship with Granny – *much Warmth in Friendship Bring*.

Thirdly and finally, when looking at the mermaid in the Pebble Alcove, he'd seen crowds of happy people on a seashore – *the Sea-people great Appear*.

That wasn't easy to work out. 'What's that to do with?'

Nigriff and Granny looked at each other. The old lady spoke first.

'It's the Alcove, and the two of us can't agree about it. Personally, I think it's you picking out the mermaid – a sea-person – and using your imagination.' Nigriff shook his head. 'But Nigriff thinks there's more to it; he reckons he's had a few odd experiences there.'

This sounded awfully familiar to Jamie. He listened carefully to Nigriff. 'My opinion may sound strange, young sir, but I wonder if there is something unusual about the building. I am sure that I once saw an image of Gulliver inside.'

Jamie sat up straight. 'Same here – that happened to me!' he exclaimed. 'Remember, Granny, I saw Gulliver tied on the cart and being towed away? You said it was because I'd been thinking about the book a lot.'

'Well, I don't know . . . really I don't. . . .' She looked sheepish; Nigriff was clearly fascinated by this piece of information.

'The trouble is,' continued Jamie, 'when I went this morning all I saw was Malplaquet. I think it's stopped working.'

'*There* you are, Nigriff,' Granny said, sounding relieved, 'it's not as weird as you think. It *is* just imagination. Jamie just needs to get the people united, not think about wacky ideas.' On that note, she folded up the old document – the discussion had come to an end. She padded back into the kitchen, leaving the other two deep in thought.

Nigriff sat silent, his arms crossed. Jamie had some sympathy for him. Granny obviously felt strongly about these matters; as far as she was concerned, there was an important job to be done, and any talk of odd buildings was an unhelpful distraction.

Jamie also wanted to be on her side. After all, he had known her for a lot longer, loved her to bits, and she was a lot bigger than Nigriff – but he didn't find her opinion about the Alcove convincing. His own experiences there had been extremely vivid, even scary. But was there any other evidence to back up Nigriff's ideas? Any other times in the gardens when his mind had played tricks on him?

And then it struck him. The afternoon before his battle with Gratton and his dog, when he had been wandering around trying to dream up a plan.

Going through the different parts of the gardens, he had come up with a whole set of different ideas, and each of them, he now realised with a shock, *matched the part he was in.* Thus when he was in Cascadia, he thought of an *athletic* plan (outrun the dog), in Elysium an *intellectual* one (persuade Gratton about canine illnesses), and then eventually in the Grecian Valley he conducted the successful *military* campaign. Somehow the character of the area, or the people in it, had affected his thinking.

Jamie felt he was on to something, but he needed to find out more. In the meantime, he was going to have to work on uniting the four groups. According to Granny, that was the Guide's main job.

Nevertheless, one other thought concerned him.

He had noticed that Pope's prophecy had plenty about fighting and battles. Neither Granny nor Nigriff had said anything about that.

Life was probably going to get even more interesting.

10: Past No More

Granny dropped the bombshell next morning immediately after breakfast. 'There's a new spirit of co-operation about,' she said happily, 'especially in my cottage. And it starts with the washing-up; I've let you off that little job too often. Even Guides have to pull their weight around the house.'

Jamie's family had a dishwasher at home, and so, to Granny's horror, he had to be shown how to actually wash dishes, and how to stack them on the draining board in a way that didn't pose a danger to Nigriff, who had to dry them. The row of upright foamy plates in their rack wasn't a great problem, but the slippery pile of cups, knives and forks, was a real Health and Safety issue.

That 'little job' took them nearly an hour. 'I'll take you to my house one day,' groaned Jamie to Nigriff, as they were both flat out in the sitting room, recovering from their exertions. 'Machines are much more civilised.'

Before Nigriff could reply, there was a knock on the window. He dived under the armchair. Jamie quickly looked round the room for anything that might give the game away – like the box containing Pope's poem! He swiftly hid it in the sideboard, then still flustered opened the door.

'Oh, it's you, Vicky. . . .' He breathed a sigh of relief. 'Hi, come in.' He shouted up the stairs behind him. 'Don't worry, Granny, it's only Vicky!' A friendly greeting was shouted back down to the newcomer, who shook the beads of rain off her hair, and fitted her coat across the back of a chair.

'Hi, Jamie. Gosh, you look exhausted! Got up too early – or too quickly?'

'Neither. Washing-up.'

'Tough life, isn't it,' she added, with a hint of sarcasm. 'Anyway, there's still a real buzz about the TQS victory. And I've got some news as well. Is Nigriff anywhere? He needs to hear it.'

A subdued Nigriff crawled out from his low hiding-place.

Vicky looked at the bedraggled figure. 'Morning. Another one worn out. . . . A new sport – Armchair Wrestling?'

'No, Miss. I am not familiar with that contest, but I'm sure that against such a static opponent, even I could record a victory.' He dusted himself down. 'No, my fatigue is due to drying the breakfast crockery and cutlery.'

'Good grief, what a pair!' laughed Vicky. 'What will happen if Granny wants the hoovering done? You'll need an ambulance!'

Jamie thought the teasing had gone far enough. 'Okay, what's your news, Vicky?'

'Oh yes, that. I've worked out something that nobody answered a few days ago.'

'I thought Nigriff and Granny told you everything?'

'Not quite. I wanted to know where the Lilliputians came from.'

'Lilliput,' said Jamie, looking at Nigriff, as if to say, 'What a stupid question. . . .'

'Yeah, I kind of worked that one out. But how did they get *here*?'

Nigriff raised his hand, as if he was answering questions in a class. 'Our records mention the possibility of a kidnap at some stage, Miss Vicky.'

'True, Nigriff. You see, I know the whole story.'

The two of them looked at her. She said two words.

'Captain Biddle.'

As soon as she spoke, Nigriff clasped a hand across his forehead and collapsed on the floor in a heap.

'Oh, my word!' shouted Vicky, shocked at the reaction. 'Quick! Mouth to mouth!'

'Don't be stupid, Vicky, you'll blow his brains out,' said Jamie, upset that she'd caused such a dramatic response in the poor chap. 'Get Granny!'

With all the commotion, the old lady was already at the bottom of the stairs. She took charge of the situation, and knelt down by Nigriff.

'Don't worry, I've seen this happen before. It's stress – he's been overdoing it. That Cup competition, I suppose.'

Jamie wondered if the drying-up could be blamed, but it wasn't the best time to say that. Granny hurried into the kitchen, returning with a damp flannel and a bicycle pump. She began dabbing at Nigriff's face and handed the pump to Jamie.

'Have a go with this – no, not in his mouth, just waft the air around his face. What brought it on anyway?'

Vicky blushed. 'It was my fault. I just said something and he keeled over.'

Granny looked up. 'Exactly *what* did you say?'

'Captain Biddle.'

Granny stopped her medical treatment and stared at Vicky. 'Who has told you about him?' There was a steely tone to her voice.

'Nobody,' said Vicky. 'I worked it out from Gulliver's Travels. I had a good look at the book again. He was the sea-captain who picked Gulliver up. I'm sure he'd have gone back to grab some people, probably to make money from them.'

Nigriff was slowly coming round, and Granny picked him up tenderly and leant him against a cushion in the armchair. Jamie and Vicky watched as she lightly smoothed his forehead, whispering quietly as she did so.

Nigriff spoke first, rather hesitantly. 'Miss Vicky, I do apologise. I didn't mean to frighten you.' He paused, taking in deep breaths of air. 'It's the name. It has lain hidden in the depths of the archives for so long. Hearing it spoken was the most enormous shock. Allow me to congratulate you on the precision of your logic.'

Granny took over. 'This isn't the time for the whole story, Vicky, but you're absolutely right. The captain was originally a good man, but he became corrupted by his dreams of easy wealth and power. He returned to the area where he'd picked up Gulliver, found Lilliput, and kidnapped a small group back to England. He wanted to lord it over his own little population. Fortunately his plans fell apart, but there was no way that his victims could ever return. The people here are the descendants of that unfortunate band.'

This deeply moved Vicky and Jamie, who felt sorry for the captain's original prisoners. 'So how did they end up at Malplaquet?'

'He used to exhibit them round the country, making them perform and do displays, and he became rich – and careless. When they came here to do their tricks for the Duke, they escaped to the island on the Eleven-Acre Lake,' continued Granny. 'As you know, they lived there undisturbed for many, many years until they had to move. The whole thing has been dreadful for them – stolen from their homeland, hiding for centuries, and now split up into separate groups!'

Jamie and Vicky now realised why Granny was so desperate for the people to forget their differences. Even Nigriff, still recovering, was moved by her final comment.

'It is desperately sad – and it is equally distressing that they have forgotten their glorious history,' he added.

'Okay,' said Jamie, 'we get the picture. So Bid . . .' and he cast an anxious glance at Nigriff.

'It's alright, sir, I can cope with the name now. It was the unexpected mention of him – Biddle, I mean. There, even I can say it. Do carry on.'

'So this Biddle is like their great enemy?'

'Not really,' said Granny calmly. 'He's long dead and buried. But he is a reminder to Nigriff and myself of this tragedy – and he represents the Lilliputians' worst fears, I suppose.'

'So they all know about him?' asked Vicky.

'Not exactly,' replied Granny. 'They think he's just a character in the old myths. I've heard parents telling naughty children, 'Just

behave or the Biddleman will get you.' No-one thinks that Captain
Biddle ever actually existed.'

'Oh no!' gasped Vicky suddenly. 'I've just remembered! Jamie
– your parents are back. I met them in the village just now. They're
coming to pick you up this afternoon.'

'I don't believe it,' groaned Jamie. 'I can't go back now.
There's far too much to be done here.'

'What are you thinking of?' asked Granny.

'Nigriff and I were talking – when we were sweating over
the dishes – about this 'mixing thing.' We want to visit another
province, like Cascadia perhaps.' Granny predictably smiled.

Vicky volunteered her help. 'I could always go with Nigriff
if Jamie can't.'

'And an even better idea,' said Granny, 'is to take the GT out
for a spin. It's got some new 'GripTread' tyres, and we could all
do with some fresh air. I'll see what I can do about your parents,
Jamie.'

As it happened, there was nothing that Granny could do this time.
His parents had really missed him whilst they were away. Back
home he went.

In Chackmore, they swapped stories about their separate
holidays. From his parents' description, France was full of quaint
villages, empty roads, historic chateaux and litres of irresistible
wine that could only be properly appreciated after the third bottle.
Jamie was enthusiastic about his time at Granny's but didn't give
away any secrets. It wasn't easy, as his Father was pumping him
for information.

'What did you learn about Landscaped Gardens?'

'Loads.'

'Such as?'

Jamie racked his brains for an answer of some sort. Far better
to say something rather than nothing. 'One bit I found out was
really interesting.'

'Which was?'

Jamie deliberately tried to be vague. 'They changed what the
gardens looked like, in the 1700s, I think.'

'Correct. How?' There was no escape on his Dad's favourite subject.

'They stopped using straight lines, and made everything curvy. More natural.'

'Splendid! Any examples?'

Jamie thought hard. This was becoming difficult. Why did grown-ups insist on making you use your brain in the summer holidays?

'Umm, not sure really . . . maybe the Octagon Lake by Granny's – it's more like a wobbly octagon nowadays. Not a proper shape.'

'Good! Sounds like you've had a useful time with her.'

And then Jamie opened his big mouth. He was never quite sure why.

'And we read some of Alexander Pope's poetry.'

This rendered his Father almost speechless. This was astonishing. His young teenage son had been reading eighteenth century poetry. All he could say was, 'Why?'

Jamie searched for an evasive answer. He tried hard but could only think of the truth. 'Because . . . it was all about Malplaquet . . . and the first Duke.'

'Ri-ight. Probably the Epistle to Lord Burlington, I would imagine,' replied his Father, pleased he could show off to his son. 'Well, it would help you to appreciate some of the finer points of the gardens, but I'm surprised that Granny would bother you with something like that. It's not easy for a boy your age to follow.'

'Some parts were easy to understand,' replied Jamie, again truthfully. 'I know a lot more about the gardens now.'

'I can see that,' said his Dad. 'Sounds like the whole visit's been a real success.'

'Definitely,' enthused Jamie. 'So when can I go back?'

'Whoa! Hang on . . . we haven't even unpacked, or picked up Charlie yet. He hasn't seen you for a while, and Granny could probably do with a rest. A couple of days here wouldn't hurt.'

'*A couple of days*? That's *ages*!' Jamie was stunned, but there was no persuading his Father otherwise. He resigned himself to his fate, dragged himself up to his bedroom and sat down at his desk, wondering how – or even *if* – the inhabitants of Malplaquet would survive if their Guide wasn't there. Anything could happen without him.

What was happening was that Granny was getting the GT out from the shed.

'What a beauty this is,' she said cheerily to Vicky and Nigriff. 'I'll give you both a lift to Venus, and then do a few laps of the lakes. Nice the weather's perking up.'

She took a sharp right off the main track and rumbled along the more wooded path by the Eleven-Acre Lake. 'We'll go this way. I've got some bread for the ducks, and it's lovely here when it's just rained.'

They stopped after a couple of minutes next to a wooden jetty, clambered out and sat on the edge of the planking. Vicky opened the bag of bread, and began to hurl a few lumps into the water.

That was when it happened.

Nigriff had lifted up a substantial crust, and was holding it with some difficulty above his head, rather like an ageing weightlifter. The load was far too heavy, and the planks were still slippery underfoot. He staggered slightly under the weight, slid a little, tried to regain his balance, put a foot out in front to steady himself . . . and a nearby duck was delighted to see a tasty-looking morsel hit the water with a loud splash and a scream.

'Bludabudlapillerblud !' he yelled, his mouth full of water. 'Help! I can't swim! Help again! Duck!' Nigriff was thrashing about, and a particularly large brown duck was swimming directly for him, head down, looking mean and hungry. It was illogical to prefer a scrawny Elysian to a fat chunk of bread, but none of those present were thinking rationally. Especially, oddly enough, Nigriff.

Before anyone could move, out from under the jetty sped a sleek wooden craft powered by a single Cascadian oarsman, straight across the line of the advancing waterfowl. The duck came to a swift halt, its wings flapping in the air as it braked, and then swam off to find another nibble. It was all over in a matter of seconds.

'Thank goodness!' said Granny with a sigh of relief. 'I'm sure that's Cyrep. Nobody else could have acted so quickly.'

The said Cascadian manoeuvred his boat alongside the gasping Nigriff, held out an oar, yanked him across the bow, and expertly rowed him back to the platform. Vicky bent over and lifted out the sodden Elysian, wrapping him in her handkerchief to keep him warm. Granny knelt down to speak with his rescuer.

'Thank you *so* much, that was extremely kind of you. He's not used to the water.'

'It was nothing. The duck wouldn't have eaten him though – not enough meat on Elysians. Mind you, the lenals aren't that fussy, and I've seen a few this summer.'

Nigriff was trying hard to listen through his shivering and the energetic rubbing that Vicky was giving him. He straightened his hair and clothes, and spoke to his rescuer.

'Please accept my warmest and wettest thanks for your timely intervention, Mr Cyrep. You have indeed confirmed what I have *always* thought about the courage and the skill of the Cascadians on the water. I will personally ensure that this noble deed will be conspicuously recorded in the Imperial Archives.'

Granny was impressed with the fulsome praise that Nigriff was handing out to another provincial. Definite progress.

'Very good of you, I'm sure,' replied Cyrep.

'Nevertheless, even though this is probably neither the time nor the place, I would like to ask *one* request of you,' added Nigriff.

'Ask away.'

'Is your boat for hire?'

Granny and Vicky were astonished. This was the very person who had just screamed that he couldn't swim, had suffered a nasty experience with the local wildlife, had always been difficult about coming near the lakes and their populations – and was now asking that particular favour?

'No, it's not for hire, none of my boats are. But if you want to have a little go in it sometime, I won't mind in the slightest.'

Nigriff was thrilled. 'Splendid. How about now?'

Granny joined in. 'Nigriff, you're soaking wet! How can you possibly go on the water like that?' She was seriously worried about his health, mental and physical.

'Madam, being wet is the ideal condition in which to go boating. In a mishap, the clothes will be well-prepared. . . . Mr Cyrep, is the boat ready for me?'

'Are you ready for the boat, sir? We'll change places and then it's all yours.'

Cyrep stepped out of his craft. The Archivist hastily clambered onto the polished seat in the centre, wobbled a bit as he settled down, and grabbed the set of oars.

'This is more like it!' he enthused. 'Anchors away!'

Cyrep opened his mouth to speak, but before he could say anything, Nigriff gave a mighty pull – and disappeared from sight as the boat shot under the jetty.

'I did wonder about him sitting that way round,' said Cyrep slowly. 'I assumed he knew what he was doing.'

'Big assumption,' said Vicky.

The three of them knelt down and tried to peer underneath. They could see very little in the gloom, but heard a familiar voice. 'Nigriff, you fool, that was reverse. Where's first gear?' There was a lot of banging and splashing, a couple of thumps as the oars hit the decking, and then Nigriff and the boat appeared from beneath their feet.

'Don't worry, good people, just getting the hang of the steering. Here we go!'

This time, the effect – and *direction* – was much more impressive. He headed out across the water with real finesse and enthusiasm.

'Never seen an Elysian row as hard as that before,' admitted Cyrep. 'In fact, come to think of it, I've never seen an Elysian row at all before. What's got into him?'

'No idea,' murmured Granny. 'He'll do himself an injury thrashing about like that.'

'Especially if he doesn't change direction,' said Vicky.

Sat with his back to the bow, Nigriff was totally unaware that

he was heading at breakneck speed towards the low bank below
the Temple of Venus. He was rowing like a man possessed, the
blades going round like windmills, great arcs of water shooting
up into the air.

'Nigriff! Stop! Put the brakes on!' screamed Vicky.

'My goodness!' shouted Granny.

'My boat!' groaned Cyrep.

Just before it hit the bank, Nigriff pulled mightily on the oars,
enough to lift the prow out of the water. The boat sped through a
narrow band of reeds, slid along the grass, and finally came to a
halt, with Nigriff thumping the blades on dry ground. He put
them down, looked around him, rubbed his hands together with
satisfaction, and hauled himself out of the boat. He greeted the
others as they came rushing over.

'*Very* nice piece of equipment, Mr Cyrep. Goes like a dream
on the water, bit sluggish on the land though. I *did* enjoy that.'

Granny didn't know what to make of it all. Nigriff getting to
know the Cascadians was one thing, in fact it was actually a
good idea, but *acting* like one was an entirely different matter.

She wished that Jamie were there. He'd understand what was
happening.

What had got into Nigriff?

11: Strange Forces

Granny had no idea what was going on, but Yenech did. He knew for certain that he had no idea where he was.

He thought there was a chance that he was in Elysium – which at least gave him the perfect opportunity to check out its curious inhabitants. Nigriff had once told him that Elysians liked to 'stretch their brains,' and 'expand their minds,' processes that to Yenech sounded fascinating (and gruesome) to watch. He was therefore hoping to bump into some of them. Which he did, by standing on someone's outstretched leg.

'Oh, I'm terribly sorry, I didn't see you sat there.'

'Evidently,' replied one of the two picnickers, sat under the edge of a jasmine bush and enjoying some refreshment. 'Yenech, I presume?'

'Er . . . yes, that's right. How did you guess? Was it the army kit?'

'That was one subtle clue,' he continued, 'and you arriving from the direction of the Grecian province was a second.'

'There are other more specific reasons,' said his companion. 'Your sense of direction is famous – you have been past this way three times already, which means I have just won a small wager – and fourthly, your meanderings fitted the name.'

Yenech stared at the landscape around him, with its gentle contours of closely mown grass, mature trees, and wide gravel paths curving past archaic monuments. It didn't look at all familiar. Had he really been this way already?

'Point five, Nigriff *has* previously described you,' explained the first speaker, 'and lastly, we ourselves saw you win the Cold Stream Cup.'

Yenech was stunned by their brilliance; they had deduced his name in *six* different ways.

'But this is most rude,' continued the Elysian. 'Let me introduce myself; I am Hondall, and this is my good friend, Mordmund. We are delighted to make your acquaintance.'

The Grecian expressed his own pleasure, and wasted no further time on formalities. 'How come you are so clever?'

'Let me explain as we return to Ancient Virtue,' replied Mordmund, packing away their refreshments in a bag. 'Do come with us; your company is light relief.'

En route they revealed one secret of their intelligence – strenuous intellectual training, such as five-a-side Chess, Karaoke Dictionary and Elysian Rules Crosswords. That final one turned out to be very complicated, with absurdly difficult answers, but there was always a hint in the clue itself. For example, *The girl at the other end (3)*, turned out to be *her*, because *her* was at the end of 'ot*her*.'

Yenech thought this silly. 'Are all the clues like that?'

'Not at all. Some work slightly differently. Let me think,' said Mordmund, nearing the Temple. 'Yenech, which cheese is made backwards?'

The question made Yenech begin to doubt this Elysian reputation for huge brainpower. Why suddenly ask about unusual food production processes? Nevertheless, he guessed at Cheddar, or Double Gloucester, but neither was correct. It was Edam.

'Why ask if you know the answer? And what's so fascinating about cheese?'

'It's another clue, Yenech. 'Edam' is the word 'made,' but backwards.' This took some explaining, illustrated with letters of twigs on the Temple steps.

'O-kay, I get the idea,' said Yenech thoughtfully, quickly adding, 'By the way, did you know that Granny is crazy?'

'That's not totally fair,' replied Mordmund. 'She says odd things at times, and her driving can be erratic, but that is a harsh judgement.'

'I couldn't agree more,' said Hondall. 'Nigriff says that she gets cross on occasion, but not too frequently.'

'Well, you're both wrong,' said Yenech, happily enjoying the moment. 'Either way you look at it, Madam is stark staring bonkers.'

The two Elysians were thoroughly perplexed. 'Would you care to explain? Why is the lady in question deranged?'

'It's logical. Madam is 'mad' from either direction. Thanks for the lesson.' And off he happily skipped towards Cascadia.

'How did all that happen?' puzzled Hondall, scratching his head.

'I haven't a clue,' said Mordmund slowly, staring after the departing figure.

The four statues of notable Greek leaders, standing high up in their own niches within the Temple of Ancient Virtue, had been following the events outside with interest. Homer, that greatest of the poets, turned his unseeing eyes towards the other three and in a low voice spoke first. 'This has all the signs of being an epic.'

Socrates, the leading philosopher, nodded his agreement. 'You speak with truth and insight. The sudden acquisition of deep wisdom by such a mortal can only be granted by the gods themselves.'

'This knowledge must be used for the good of all the people,' declared Lycurgus of Sparta, the wisest law-maker in the ancient world. 'It will require people of considerable ability and strength of character.'

'Therefore it is fortunate indeed that at least this Yenech has been trained in the military arts,' added the fourth figure – Epaminondas, the famous and respected Theban general. 'It is a proven fact that soldiers make the best leaders.'

The others were on the point of discussing this controversial statement with him when in walked an older couple, their dog straining on its lead. Conversation immediately ceased, and the ivory-coloured statues became as motionless and as silent as ever. Another of their frequent and incisive debates would have to wait for a more convenient time.

That same evening Nigriff was leaving Granny's cottage when he saw Vicky inside the Lake Pavilion. She was sat with her head in her hands, deep in thought. This bothered him, so with a great effort he clambered up the steps. Vicky didn't see him until he was right by her feet.

'Oh, sorry, Nigriff. I was miles away.'

'You may well have been, Miss Vicky. But now you are here. Is there anything I can help you with?

'I don't know. It's a big problem. It's Yenech.'

Nigriff hesitated. 'Hmm. He has always been a grave concern. The General is aware of the difficulty, though he has some good points. His running, for example. . . .'

'No, Nigriff, this is much more serious. He's changed. He's gone all brainy.'

Nigriff was noticeably shocked. 'That is *very* alarming. However, it may perhaps be only a temporary relapse – normal functioning might be restored soon. What are the main symptoms of his unfortunate disorder?'

'I just met him in Cascadia, going on about clues, and words spelt backwards, and words inside other words. It was really odd.'

Nigriff became thoughtful and spoke slowly. 'Would you say it's as odd as an unfit Archivist, with a highly developed sports phobia, setting a new twenty-metre rowing record on water *and* dry land?'

When Vicky said a simple, 'Yes,' that was enough for Nigriff.

'I knew it,' he said grimly. 'It is time for another talk with Madam. This is precisely what I have suspected all along. It *is* actually happening, just as the prophecies said. Come, we must hurry.'

The meeting between the three of them was brief but to the point. Nigriff was adamant. He insisted that these two recent cases of extreme character changes led to only one possible conclusion – something was altering their behaviour in different parts of the garden. In Cascadia, he himself had suddenly developed amazing athletic qualities; in Elysium, Yenech had inexplicably started to become an intellectual. The evidence seemed undeniable.

'But why is it only happening now?' asked Vicky in bewilderment.

'The Lilliputians have been used to staying pretty much in their own areas,' suggested Granny. 'So they've stayed as particular types. Perhaps if they move around, they'll begin to copy the others. Like Yenech. He's been all over Malplaquet. Maybe that's why he's so mixed-up. . . . '

'Another explanation might be more dramatic,' suggested Nigriff. 'Some might say that Master Jamie's arrival has disturbed our world's order.' He couldn't help but recall the good old days of meeting only intellectuals in Elysium.

'Do you mean like an Immortal in the Greek myths, Nigriff?' said Vicky. 'You know, coming down to earth and upsetting things?'

'Not the Greek myths, Miss Vicky, but the Malplaquet ones, the Writings.' Once Nigriff had said that, he had to explain about Pope's poem and Jamie being the Guide. Vicky was impressed – especially by Jamie matching the Three Tests. 'I should have realised something was going on when he was chatting to that rabbit a couple of weeks ago,' she said. 'Or maybe he hasn't told you about that. . . . Anyway, it's obvious what we've got to do now.'

'It is?' asked Granny.

'Of course. We need to tell him what we think is going on – unless he's worked it out for himself. Come on – let's ring him.'

Whilst Jamie was talking on the phone, his Mum was dusting the other end of the hall. He didn't want to arouse her suspicions, and he was speaking as quietly as he could, but it was difficult with an old lady who lacked perfect hearing. Another problem was that Jamie couldn't help reacting to the news.

'*He fell in*? Throwing a lump of bread . . . ? But he can't swim. . . . And a duck was about to eat him. . . ? But he's never rowed before. Crashed by Venus? Lost again – and his brain's bigger?' Mrs. Thompson was suddenly cleaning right by him. Jamie finished the call rapidly – 'Sorry, Granny, must go,' – and slammed the phone down.

Mrs. Thompson decided he looked guilty. 'So *who* is this boy then? I thought you'd only seen Granny and Vicky?'

Jamie thought it best to tell the truth, as calmly as possible.

'He's a little chap who lives nearby. He pops in to see Granny sometimes.'

'He fell in the lake?'

'Ye-es, it sounds like it.'

'And he was nearly eaten by a duck?'

'Well, those ducks can be funny when they're hungry. And he's quite small.'

'He crashed a boat onto the bank?' Jamie nodded.

'I'm beginning to get worried about Granny's state of mind,' continued Mum. 'She allows a little boy – who can't swim – to fall in a lake, get attacked by the wildfowl, and to be in charge of a boat that he wrecks. It wasn't your new boat, was it? And is the poor chap still alive?'

'No, it wasn't mine, and Granny said he's *really* alive.'

Mum stared at Jamie in blank disbelief, trying to find the words. 'I daren't ask about his bigger brain either,' she said in a daze, shaking her head.

'So when can I go back?' asked Jamie. Not the right question. No answer.

'That wasn't much help,' admitted Granny, putting the phone down. 'Somebody's going to have to go and see him.'

'Sounds like me,' said Vicky. 'Nigriff can't stand on his doorstep and ask if Jamie can come out to play. It's too late now though – I'll go tomorrow morning.'

Jamie was lying on his bed, very bored, staring blankly up at the ceiling as the morning sunlight poured in through the window. He had worked out that eighteen hours had passed; with any luck he had served half his sentence. Would his parents let him out early for good behaviour? Then he heard them talking downstairs, Mum's voice first.

'All I can say is that I'm worried. He's not been the same since he came back.'

'Of course he isn't – he's growing up. He's had a fun time with her, and now it's back to boring old home.'

'Well, I think she's been spoiling him. I dread to think the stories she's been filling his mind with – never mind all those pancakes for breakfast. I told you last night about that poor little boy and his boat. We shouldn't have left him with her for that long. Babysitting's one thing, but. . . .'

'I'm sure it was perfectly harmless. All he's been doing is running around a huge garden for a couple of weeks. Some kids his age spend most of their holidays on the streets, bumping into all sorts of strange characters. He's been well away from that – he won't have seen anybody apart from Granny and Vicky.'

'That doesn't bother me. It's the fact he's gone really quiet – and don't you think it's odd getting into old poetry? How many boys do you know who want to read "anything by Alexander Pope"? He should be doing something active at his age.'

'But aren't you pleased he's got an academic hobby? Isn't it better than just kicking a football around?'

'If it *was* just a hobby, that would be fine, but it's more like an obsession. Look at his bedroom floor – covered in bits of cardboard from those models he's making. These gardens aren't doing him any good. Where's it all going to lead?'

'Exactly,' mused Jamie. 'What *is* going on at Malplaquet?'

A loud ring on the doorbell interrupted his train of thought. He heard the latch being lifted, the door squeak open, and then, much to his surprise and relief, Vicky's voice.

'Hello, Mrs. Thompson, is Jamie in?'

'Yes, he is, Vicky, but he's having a quiet day today. I think he's been overdoing it recently, to be honest. But I suppose five minutes wouldn't do any harm. He's in his room.' Footsteps tapped up the stairs, and then Vicky's smiling face peered round the door, greeting him cheerily. 'Hi there – how is the long-awaited Guide?'

'Shh! Keep your voice down, Vicky! So they told you?'

'Dead impressed – pity you didn't know much about Pope though.'

'I knew things about *other* popes. Anyway, what's the news? Is that right about Nigriff and Yenech?'

She confirmed what Granny had said on the phone. 'Definitely weird. Not at all like them.'

'You've all talked about it?'

'Yes, but we can't totally agree. Granny realises the place is probably more peculiar than she thought, but you know what Nigriff's like, always on about forces and things like that. He reckons something in a province can affect people.'

'He's right!' exclaimed Jamie, desperately trying to keep his voice down. 'Honest. It happened to me.' He explained his experiences when he was thinking how to beat Gratton and his dog. 'It's freaky. What do you reckon?'

'I'm sure something's going on – but it's *your* opinion that matters the most,' she replied, adding half-teasingly, 'O True Source of all Pure Knowledge and Insight.'

Jamie took a swipe at her with his pillow, just as the cry came from downstairs, 'Visiting hours over!' He went to the door with Vicky, adding, 'Look, I should be back tomorrow. We'll sort something out then.'

'Okay, but I want to chat about the Alcove as well. It sounds bizarre.'

'Sure – but don't expect any answers. Say 'Hi' to Granny and Nigriff and the others.'

'Will do,' said Vicky, and she was gone.

Jamie sat on the edge of his bed. Things were complicated, even confusing. He looked at the model of Malplaquet he'd started. The large piece of chipboard had been cut to the shape of the gardens, and he'd marked in paths and lakes. He'd even drawn in the outlines of some buildings, such as the Temple of Venus, near to where Nigriff had become a supreme oarsman. The Temple of Ancient Virtue, where Yenech had understood crosswords. The Greek Temple, where he himself had fought Gratton.

As he looked, something clicked, and an extraordinary idea began to form in his mind. 'It's not just the provinces,' breathed Jamie slowly, 'It's. . . .'

'Lunchtime,' interrupted Charlie, his head poking round the door. 'Mum says you've got to come now, and stop making a mess with all the cardboard.' Jamie didn't feel irritated by his brother. He had just come to a really interesting conclusion.

'Don't know what to do with him, Miss. Strangest thing that I've seen in all my years in the army. Had a case a bit like it once on the northwest frontier, lonely place, turns people's heads, hallucinations, nothing as bad as this though.' General Thorclan was discussing with Vicky the sad case of Yenech. They were sat at the far end of the Grecian valley, looking back down its length towards the Temple and the setting sun. He continued his lament. 'I don't know where he got the idea from, playing around with words and letters. And as for our temple inscription – that word *Victoriae*. He thinks it means you, not Victory. He's lost it.'

'I think it's sweet, General, just a bit of fun. Don't take it too seriously.'

'But it's not just that – all these crosswords? The world's gone mad. Thank goodness our army can still guard Malplaquet, even in Master Jamie's absence.'

'He'll return as soon as he can,' replied Vicky. 'I had a chat with him this morning; his Mum said he's got to stay at home for a while.'

As they sat there, enjoying the peace of the early evening, they suddenly noticed a lone visitor wandering along the path amongst the bushes to their right. He was dressed in a long dark coat, which was unusual given that it had been a fine August day. He was walking very slowly, stopping every now and again, and consulting a large book that he was carrying. Round his neck was slung a pair of binoculars.

'He's a late visitor,' muttered Vicky to Thorclan, who was already climbing inside her bag. 'He should have gone by now. Perhaps he's to do with the restoration.'

'Maybe,' answered a muffled voice, 'but don't panic.'

Vicky watched as the man drew nearer to her, clearly intending to talk. In spite of the good military advice she felt nervous, and as he got closer she was shaken by his appearance. Apart from the overcoat, which was torn around the pockets and badly faded, his shoes were well-worn and split across the front. His skin was pale and tired, and his hair had been neither cut nor washed for many weeks, reminding her of greasy seaweed. Even at a distance he smelt, of something earthy, like compost. When only a step away, he parted his lips in a thin and unattractive smile.

'Good evening, young lady,' he purred, in a polished and posh accent, 'isn't this the most perfect setting?'

'Er, yes.' Vicky wasn't expecting such a polite introduction.

'I am constantly amazed at the splendour of these grounds. One never knows what one might see.' Vicky silently agreed. She felt movement in her bag. 'This book is such a splendid help.' He opened it up near the back. 'Is that not a delightful picture of the Triumphal Arch?'

Vicky glanced at it, a full-colour drawing of what she knew as the Corinthian Arch, built on the skyline facing the South Front. 'It's nice.'

'Indeed it is. These gardens are full of wonders, all sorts of little things that most people don't notice.' He turned his head towards her and leaned over, too close for Vicky's liking. 'I don't suppose you've come across anything like that, have you?' She shook her head, afraid to say anything in case he detected her nervousness. He paused before continuing. 'Hmm. Pity. I thought perhaps you might have done. Anyway, I'm afraid I must depart. I do hope to see you again.' He sidled off, leaving Vicky feeling cold and frightened. Did he know something? And why was such a well-spoken man dressed as badly that?

Thorclan pushed his head and shoulders out of the bag.

'Good grief, I could smell the man from in here. My officers would sort the fellow out. You'd soon see what we'd make of him.'

'I'd be happy never to see him again in my whole life,' shuddered Vicky. 'He gave me the creeps. C'mon, let's go back; it's turned chilly. Maybe Yenech is at the Temple. I'll ask him about my inscription. . . .'

12: Restoring the Temples

'Morning, Granny,' called out Mr. Thompson, as the car slowed to a halt by her gate, 'I've returned your assistant.'

Granny was leaning against the back door, putting on her outdoor shoes. Hearing that description of Jamie, she shot a quick glance at him. Had he told his Father something? Jamie shook his head discreetly, and heaved a rucksack and his model of Malplaquet from the car.

'Oh yes, good morning – and to you, Charlie. I haven't seen you for ages.'

'When is it my turn?' asked Charlie. 'Jamie's been here lots.'

'Charlie, I said not to ask,' said Dad. 'It's up to Granny if she wants you.'

Granny smiled at the young boy. 'You're right, Charlie,' she said. 'It is about time. Tell you what, let me get the spare bed sorted out and a few things moved round, then I'll give your Mum a ring. I do keep my guests busy though.'

'I don't mind,' said Charlie. 'It's better than being on my own at home.'

'Right then,' said Dad breezily, 'we'll leave you to it. Be good, Jamie. See you soon.' To Granny's delight, he gave her a goodbye peck on both cheeks (a new habit from France, thought Jamie), and then drove up the track, Charlie's face staring out of the rear window. He was grinning at his brother, and feeling very satisfied.

Jamie didn't mind, he was just glad to be back. The gardens as always seemed like home, where he could be himself. It was becoming hard to imagine anywhere else mattering so much to him.

Granny interrupted his thoughts. 'Lovely to have you here, Jamie. We've missed you.' They gave each other a hug. 'Actually, you just caught me,' she said. 'This thing about the people changing is a bit strange, we need to know if it's happening to others. Can you look after yourself for a while?' Jamie nodded. 'Good. You'll find a little something in the kitchen.' She pushed open the Bell Gate and wandered off.

As Granny had hinted, Nigriff was inside. Panicking at the sound of footsteps on the path, he had scrambled into a box of breakfast cereal lying on its side. Realising it was only Jamie, he crawled out, grasping a few lumps of Bran Flakes.

'Good morning, sir, how are you? None the worse for your absence, I presume?'

'I'm fine, Nigriff. Are *you* okay? I hear you've been up to all sorts of tricks. Competing with Cascadians?'

'Indeed, sir. It has been most enlightening. There is much to be said for this exercise idea; being fit is such an intelligent thing to do.'

'Is that why you're into breakfast?'

'Absolutely, sir. Your grandmother ascribes remarkable qualities to these Flakes. She says they keep her going all day. They are just what I need.'

'They might help your running, I suppose. Anyway, come and see what I've got. It might turn you into a Grecian *and* a Cascadian.'

As Jamie unpacked his bag, the Archivist's eyes opened wide. 'Rentur the Wise!' exclaimed Nigriff. 'Is that fearsome weapon legal?'

Jamie was lovingly handling a toy crossbow, made of bright red plastic. It fired plastic arrows, tipped with black rubber suckers, and in Nigriff's world, in the wrong hands, it would undoubtedly do serious damage.

'You might find this fun,' said Jamie eagerly. 'Let's put up some targets.'

'*Targets*, Master Jamie? Who are you thinking of?'

'Don't worry, Nigriff, they're just footballers I collect.'

Jamie delved into his bag and pulled out the figures. He lined up ten of them on the wall – all about half the size of Nigriff, with disproportionately big heads.

The Elysian was impressed by the models. 'Judging by the extra size of their craniums, sir, these people are endowed with awesome brain capacities. Elysians I assume?'

'Er . . . maybe a couple,' said Jamie hesitantly. 'Anyway, let's see what you can do.' He outlined the weapon's main features, and because the weight and size made it impossible for Nigriff to hold it firmly, they set it up wedged between some bricks. Jamie also set the string back in position after each shot, as it was far too tight for a tiny person to pull. Eventually Nigriff was able with a huge effort to release the trigger, and he did actually twice fire an arrow. The first time, he hit a figure in a grey suit.

'There goes the manager,' said Jamie. 'Another one fired.'

The second arrow hit a figure wearing a pink halter-neck top and sunglasses.

'Vicky!' shouted Jamie, genuinely pleased, and he rushed over to greet her. He wanted to kiss her on both cheeks like his Dad, but he just gave her a quick hug instead. 'Thanks for coming to see me yesterday. Granny's gone for a short walk to check out any more changes. I'm turning Nigriff into a Grecian.'

'That *would* be a miracle,' said Vicky, smiling at the Archivist. 'Maybe we should leave him in the Grecian Valley to see if that does the job?'

Nigriff looked shocked at the prospect, and was relieved when Jamie said, 'I don't think that's *exactly* how it works, Vicky. I've had one or two other ideas.'

'Sounds interesting,' said Vicky, 'but I want to check out the Pebble Alcove with you first. You can tell me on the way.'

'Fine,' agreed Jamie. 'Nigriff, you hold the fort. Have some more breakfast.'

Nigriff, although obviously reluctant to be a full Grecian, was nevertheless pleased at being left on guard. 'Could I really become a *regular* soldier, sir?'

'Keep eating those Bran Flakes and it's very likely,' replied Jamie, and he and Vicky headed off, leaving behind a puzzled Elysian.

'So you've seen all sorts of things in here – like the seaside?' The two were standing outside the Alcove.

Jamie nodded. 'That was in the Tests, then the next time I saw a huge man – Gulliver probably – being towed away on a massive cart. After that it didn't seem to work, and all I saw was Malplaquet.'

'Maybe you didn't do something in the correct order – or you weren't in the right mood,' said Vicky thoughtfully. She nudged him forward. 'Go on, there's no point in hanging around.'

Jamie took a deep breath, walked forward, sat on the bench, and let his eyes drift over the shapes. He was drawn to a pair of inter-connecting circles, one slightly bigger than the other. At once the light mist descended again, and on its screen he was staring at a solid iron circle, a manacle that was fitting tightly around someone's left ankle and then attached by its chain to a wall. The person couldn't move far. Jamie felt scared, almost as if he was the prisoner; quickly the mist cleared to reveal Vicky, looking anxiously at him.

'What was it?' she said. 'You seemed really worried.'

'It was working again. Someone had been captured,' said Jamie nervously. 'They couldn't walk because their leg was tied up. It felt like it was me.'

'I bet I know what it is,' she stated confidently. 'It's Gulliver again. You know, when he was taken to the capital and slept inside that huge building. They used loads of chains and padlocks to make sure he wouldn't escape.'

Jamie was shaken by how realistic the image had been. 'Granny says it's only because I've got the book on the brain. But it's not just thinking, I can feel it.'

'Does it work with anybody else?' asked Vicky.

Jamie didn't know. 'Nigriff reckons he's seen some vague things in there, but I'm not sure about others.'

'Shall I have a try?'

Jamie shrugged his shoulders. 'I suppose so. Check out the mermaid first.'

Vicky looked up at the figure outlined in pebbles. The way she described it afterwards, a grey watery shadow appeared across the entrance and she might have seen a beach, and maybe some people – but it was all rather vague. Jamie agreed that it sounded just like his Third Test. At least they knew that the Alcove was still working.

Returning to the cottage, they found Granny by her table looking subdued, holding a cup of tea. Nigriff was seated on the polished surface facing her.

'Oh good, you're here,' she said. 'I was getting worried.'

'We're fine, Granny,' said Vicky, 'nothing much could have happened to us.'

'Well, I can't say the same about the Lilliputians,' she muttered. 'I've just been telling Nigriff. Some very strange goings-on.' She sipped at her tea.

Jamie sat down next to her. 'Like what?'

'It's happening, exactly as Nigriff said.'

'What – more people *are* changing?' asked Vicky.

'Everywhere, lots of them.' She sighed. 'I thought there might be one or two, but . . . I had a chat with Nivloc's Mum. Lovely Elysian lad, always interested in ancient myths, went for a swim recently in the Indoor Pool in Cascadia, and now he's sports mad. Plays tennis all the time.' She shook her head. 'And Hamnob, a delightful Palladian girl. Always good company, so loyal to her parents, and what happens? Helps Yenech find his way back to the Grecian Temple – and then returns home, declaring she's going to start military training. Broken her Mum's heart it has.'

Nigriff interrupted this tale of woe. 'It's not *all* bad news, Madam. What about the Cascadian Atose, famed for his skill with a ball, who met a girl at Ancient Virtue, and has now found a love for books? Surely that has to be a good development?'

Granny tried to agree, but she was still upset. 'I didn't want to believe you, but you're right; something odd is affecting the people. They're becoming all mixed-up, confused. It's not what I hoped for.' Tears began.

Jamie took her hand in his. He was smiling. 'Granny, can't you see, this is *exactly* what you wanted? They're not getting *mixed-up*, they're getting united – becoming one people again.' There was a note of real excitement in his voice. 'It's far better than just getting on with each other; they're actually losing their differences.'

The old lady looked at him in astonishment. 'Are you saying this is the prophecy?'

'I'm sure of it,' said Jamie. 'And there's something else. I haven't told the others yet.' Nigriff and Vicky stared at him. 'It was after your visit, Vicky, and you'd mentioned about Yenech and Nigriff behaving oddly. When you left, I was looking at my model, thinking about exactly where they'd been at the time.'

'In Cascadia and Elysium, you mean?' said Vicky.

'No, no, more *precise* than that,' replied Jamie, choosing his words carefully. 'They were near two Temples – Venus and Ancient Virtue. And did you notice about the people Granny just mentioned? They were close to buildings as well.'

The other three looked at each other quizzically.

Vicky broke the silence first. 'So you reckon it's more to do with the temples than the provinces?' Jamie nodded. 'I think so. If you hang around in a province you change gradually, but near the old monuments you change really quickly.'

Nigriff had been sat quietly, listening carefully, but now he spoke. 'These are extraordinary claims, Master Jamie, but your logic appears sound. If I could mention a question of mine, is it reasonable to assume that the Pebble Alcove is like the others, and that some force is focussed there?'

'Definitely,' said Jamie. 'And another thing, it's working again. Vicky and I tried it out just now. I got a really strong picture, and even Vicky saw something. It's still showing bits of the Gulliver story.'

'This is *most* remarkable,' exclaimed Nigriff. 'A new type of archive – even more exciting than shelves of documents. Living *pictures*, not words!'

These conclusions were almost too much to take in, but the events of the summer now were making sense. Whatever influence was at work in the gardens seemed stronger around the temples, and it was causing the Lilliputians to lose their provincial differences. In the Alcove it also showed their ancient history. All this coincided with Pope's Guide appearing – Jamie, becoming a man at age thirteen.

Then a sudden thought struck Nigriff. 'They are in the poem.'

'What are?' asked Granny.

'Temples restored,' explained Nigriff. 'In the new Empire.'

'So what does that mean?' asked Granny.

'One can at present only state the obvious, that many buildings are being restored. There must be a connection.' He spoke quietly but firmly. 'And on the same topic, I should again raise the issue of the Forces of Restoration and Destruction.' The other two looked mystified. Granny explained. 'It's from another old writing, about the Empire becoming strong, and good and bad things happening together.'

'In the light of these developments and our consequent deliberations,' concluded Nigriff importantly, 'I feel that we have a duty to inform the proper authorities; in other words we need to speak to the Assembly. We have some compelling evidence, so we should act promptly.'

Before anyone could respond, the phone rang and made them all jump. Granny padded to the kitchen to answer it, and on her return announced the news. 'Charlie's coming after lunch. Apparently he's been a nuisance all morning, I can't put him off any longer. He's stopping the night as well.'

Jamie groaned. Exactly what they didn't need at this critical time.

This was incredibly annoying.

The car drew up in the middle of the afternoon. An apologetic Dad came in, pushing a grinning Charlie in front of him. 'I'm sorry about this, Granny, but he thinks he's being left out. Hello, Vicky, how are you?'

In spite of the frustration that everyone else was feeling, Granny was her usual welcoming self. 'Oh, don't worry, it's no trouble at all. Come on, I've got some things ready – juice for the boys, and I'm sure nobody would say no to a biscuit or two.'

Jamie gave his younger brother a hard stare as they sat down. There was an awkward silence in the room. Dad tried to encourage a more positive atmosphere.

'Well, Granny, I must say I was amazed to hear you've introduced Jamie to Alexander Pope. Goodness, are you alright?'

Granny had spluttered into her tea, spilling half of it in her saucer and showering the chair with soggy biscuit crumbs. Dad passed her a tea towel, and Jamie intervened quickly. 'It was just one poem, about the first Duke, wasn't it, Granny?'

She nodded, wiping her mouth and trying to collect her thoughts. 'Mmm,' she agreed, swallowing stray bits of biscuit, 'we came across it one day, and I was telling Jamie what I knew about it.'

'Presumably the one to Lord Burlington, the *second* of Pope's Moral Essays?' inquired Dad, keen to show off his knowledge. Granny now realised, to her horror, that Jamie's Dad knew a fair bit about the author. She didn't want to reveal anything about the poem, so she tried to deflect his interest.

'No, no, it wasn't that one. I think it was the *fifth*, if I remember correctly.' She calmly sipped what was left of her drink.

It was now Mr. Thompson's turn to react. 'The *Fifth*! Are you sure? You've seen it? Where?'

Granny coughed furiously into her tea, and the little that had been left suddenly appeared in a small cascade over the edge.

'Dad,' interrupted Jamie, aware that she had unintentionally provoked further interest, 'it *can't* have been that. You're right – *must* have been the second.'

'I'd be very surprised if it was the Fifth,' he replied. 'I know you've got lots of old books and documents lying around here, but Pope's missing Fifth Essay is one of the great mysteries of English Literature. It's like the search for the Holy Grail . . . or the lost city of Atlantis . . . or. . . .'

'Elvis' brain?' offered Charlie, trying to contribute to an adult conversation. They all turned towards him.

Kasuya immediately sprinted away like a shot.

'Not exactly . . . ' said his Dad. 'No, the search for the Fifth Moral Essay has been plaguing academics for nearly three centuries. There are rumours that he wrote a fifth and final one to Burlington, with the hope of untold wealth to whoever interpreted the poem correctly. 'Pope's treasure' they call it. Sadly, we don't know if it exists or not. Some Oxford professors have spent their whole academic careers looking for it.'

'*Definitely* wasn't that one,' said Jamie emphatically, whose heart had missed a beat at the mention of untold wealth.

'Absolutely,' said Granny. 'There aren't many riches here.'

'And not many brains,' muttered Charlie to himself. He was already thinking that Jamie must have had a really weird couple of weeks, looking for possibly lost bits of poetry with an old lady who sprayed her friends with tea and biscuits.

'Anyway, I need to get back,' said Mr. Thompson, glancing at his watch. 'Are you sure you're okay with Charlie? I'll pick him up first thing in the morning.'

'He'll be fine as usual,' replied Granny, putting an arm round him. 'I'm going to treat him just as I did Jamie. We'll have a grand tour – Palladian Bridge, Chinese House, Friendship . . . Shouldn't take more than two hours.'

With that, she swept out the door, bustling Charlie and his Dad ahead of her.

'Thank goodness Granny's on the ball,' said Jamie to Vicky. 'Now Charlie's out of the way, we can think about what to do next. And he's going back tomorrow. Maybe we can get an Assembly called after all.'

As it happened, they didn't need to. During that very afternoon, one particular Elysian, Kasuya, who had a fondness for afternoon siestas, was enjoying his usual slumber under a bush behind Ancient Virtue. He was shaken out of his repose by a little girl, aged about seven, who was leaning over him shouting, 'Mum! Dad! Come and see! There's a tiny person asleep here!' Kasuya immediately sprinted off like a shot, and luckily the parents were the sensible sort who didn't believe her but were nevertheless pleased with their daughter's developing powers of imagination.

Clearly this was a new development. For decades, the tiny inhabitants of Malplaquet had been pretty much invisible to all humans; they had, as it were, *melted* into the landscape after their arrival. The present population knew that only a very small handful of humans (who 'lived and breathed' the gardens like Jamie and Granny) were able to see them. Of course, they had always taken very careful precautions, but to the vast majority of the human race, they were no more than shadows or vague misty shapes. Their movements had usually been mistaken for a trick of the light, or small animals in the undergrowth, or maybe the wind rustling the leaves.

They had been extremely safe. But all that seemed to have changed.

The fact that a casual visitor could so easily and blatantly spot the dozing Kasuya was intensely frightening to the Lilliputian population. For many it could only mean that something – or some*one* – had upset the balance of nature in Malplaquet.

The news of it spread rapidly and almost triggered an immediate panic.

The Listener had no alternative.

She summoned an 'Extraordinary Provincial Assembly' to convene at the earliest possible opportunity.

13: An Extraordinary Assembly

It was not a great evening. Vicky went home for supper, Jamie thought about what he would be doing if Charlie wasn't around, and Charlie himself seemed determined to be difficult. He was hopeless at washing-up (spoilt by the dishwasher, reckoned Jamie), messed up the bedroom with his clobber, was rude about Jamie's model buildings . . . and then there was Scrabble.

The trouble of course was that Jamie, with Nigriff's help, had been learning some interesting new words over the summer. Granny realised the problem when Jamie put down 'LENAL' and Charlie fell about laughing.

'You can't put that!' he sniggered. 'What's a lenal?'

'It's a fish, a vicious one,' responded Jamie. 'Some people call them vazedirs. They're in the lakes here.'

'Don't be stupid,' said Charlie. 'Granny, tell him he can't have that.'

To Jamie's dismay, she took Charlie's side. 'It's a foreign word, Jamie,' she said knowingly. 'Or is it a local dialect? Anyway, I'm afraid you can't play it.'

Jamie felt like saying, 'We did last time,' but he knew what she meant. In the end, he had to suffer Charlie beating him – all the more frustrating when he'd once had exactly the right letters to make 'LUSHOYE' (a spider's web gleaming with dew, often pointed out by Nigriff), which would have scored eighty points.

Life simply wasn't fair at times – and then the milk ran out that evening.

The following morning when Jamie woke, he still felt under a cloud. He dressed, filled a bowl with cereal and then remembered the lack of milk. Really annoying. He thought that getting out might change his mood, and in the back yard he spotted his crossbow and arrows; he picked them up and set off.

All was quiet by the Octagon. The ducks on the water were drifting around looking fast asleep, cows were steadily chewing in the nearest field, and in the distance he could see a couple of people out walking their dogs. In some ways it was a very typical and placid August morning.

Jamie's mind, however, was in turmoil. He was irritated by his brother's intrusion, and bothered by Nigriff's fears about likely conflict. 'Restoration and Destruction' – what sort of trouble could be meant? He fired off an arrow. It went further than he'd intended, and plopped into the water. 'Just my luck,' he thought.

His circuit of the lake took him longer than usual. He tried to find some sticks for whittling into arrows once he was back at Granny's, and he also set up some fir-cone targets on a tree-stump. Suddenly spotting his Father's car pull up by the cottage, he realised that he must have been out for ages. 'At least Charlie's going soon,' he thought. 'Then we can carry on.' He continued to dawdle along, not bothered about saying goodbye to his brother.

The route took him across the Palladian Bridge and through the province itself. He lost his final arrow aiming at some large seed-cases on a tree – it ricocheted off and disappeared into long grass at the water's edge. 'Stupid thing!' said Jamie angrily, hurling his crossbow after it, and then taking a bad-tempered kick at a loose stone. His foul mood was interrupted by a familiar voice.

'Thank goodness, there you are! We've been looking for you everywhere!'

Granny was at the wheel of her GT, waving frantically. The car did a slow-motion version of screeching to a halt. Nigriff was sat in the front holding on to the seat belt for dear life, his arms and legs wrapped around the fabric. Jamie could see they were both extremely worried; maybe it was her driving.

'The Listener has called a special assembly for all the PRs, we haven't had one of those for years, and we've no idea what it's about,' blurted out Granny. 'She's said that *you* have to be there, Nigriff found out this morning.'

'Master Jamie,' panted Nigriff, his face pale and anxious, 'this may be bad news. We should get there as soon as possible.'

Jamie didn't feel like hurrying. He ambled over. 'Why should it be *bad* news? I'm usually there anyway, I'm a fringe member.'

'Indeed sir, but this time she is *adamant* that you attend. I'm not happy about how this has occurred – without warning, and with little historical precedent. I must insist, sir, that you join us in the vehicle. All haste to the Gothic Temple, Madam, and don't spare the horses!'

So off they sped, with Granny pressing the pedal to the floor to achieve its top velocity of slightly above walking pace, and Jamie thinking that one day soon he must explain to Nigriff the proper terms for various forms of transport.

Despite their rapid progress, they were the last to arrive. Granny said it was clearly such a special meeting, that it was best if she didn't come in without a specific invitation; she would see them later.

Jamie and Nigriff made their way towards the closed door – solid and ancient, covered in black knobbly bolt-heads. Nigriff knocked, firmly but not aggressively.

It was opened, slowly and with difficulty, by Yeda, an Elysian PR who was an old friend of Nigriff's. He was embarrassed, and spoke in an awkward manner. 'Oh, it's you, Nigriff, good. You'd best come in . . . both of you, I suppose.'

The two followed him into the central circular room. They had gone no more than a few paces when a sharp voice echoed across the stone floor. It was the Listener.

'Yeda! I said *he* was to be shown upstairs. He's not a fringe member in *this* debate.'

Yeda turned to Jamie. 'I'm awfully sorry, sir, but those are my orders. I can't let you come any further. The Upper Gallery, please. I am sorry.' Perplexed, Jamie made his way up the spiral staircase to the first floor.

He stepped out onto the landing that ran all round the inside of the single room, its splendid domed ceiling covered in glittering mosaic crests. This public area was packed full of spectators, peering through the balustrade, but to Jamie's surprise they were standing in four *separate* groups. He instantly took this division as a bad sign, a return to their old ways. As he slowly inched forward, nobody greeted him, but two groups parted to give him some space, as if wanting nothing to do with him. Not a word was spoken, but every eye was on Jamie. The atmosphere was uncomfortable and tense. He caught sight of Nigriff below, seated amongst the Elysian PRs on the rug. He was being given the same frosty welcome, and was nervously looking around.

The Listener, standing behind three books laid flat on their sides, spoke first.

'As you know, this chamber has heard many reasoned and careful debates in its history,' she boomed. 'Our democratic processes in framing our laws have led to this Assembly being held in the highest regard. Today we are holding an *Extraordinary* Assembly, one *so* extraordinary, that I am using the powers vested in me to transform this meeting into a lawcourt. We will not be *making* laws, but *judging* by the law.'

Nigriff turned to search for Jamie's face. White as a sheet (and much bigger than anyone else's), it wasn't difficult to pick out. The solemn introduction continued. 'We have been living through exciting times, bringing many changes. Some of us were pleased, and some of us were, shall I say, *apprehensive*. But we waited . . . waited to see if the changes were for the better. The time for waiting is now over.' A couple of PRs stamped their feet. 'This morning in my house, before first light, I met a number of the leading Representatives and we drew up a list of accusations – I beg your pardon, *concerns*. I shall read them, one at a time, for your careful consideration.'

'Can we vote now?' piped up one PR (Thema, Palladian).

'Do I *really* have to repeat myself?' The icy tone answered her own question. 'This is not a normal Assembly, but a courtroom. Proper legal processes *will* be followed; there will be no vote – at least, not yet. *Do* pay attention!' She shuffled her papers and laid them on her desk of books. 'Each accusation – or concern – will be introduced by a PR, then there will be an opportunity for others to add further information. Once the list is finished, we will consider the suitable penalty.' There were murmurs of approval. Jamie was now starting to panic; what had happened to make them so hostile?

'The first charge; that the Assistant Guide, a Mr. James Thompson, has *Seriously Diluted the Cultural and Sporting Heritage of our Peoples*. Proposed by Maneroc of Cascadia.'

Maneroc, a noted Cascadian runner, spoke with much emotion on the good old days of the Cold Stream Cup, when events unfolded with regularity. It was no longer the same, he argued. The winners could not be predicted, and the new trend for mixed teams was a dangerous tendency – no *one* province would be confident of winning, and therefore many wouldn't bother to train at all.

The Listener seemed impressed – at least that was a reasonable assumption from her applause as Maneroc resumed his seat. Her words led to the same conclusion. 'An *excellent* start. Would others like to add more?'

Thims, a Palladian who had competed in the Cup this year, performing creditably on the Water Crossing, rose to his feet. 'Madam Listener, I would do so, but it might fit the next charge better.'

'No, now is the best time. Which one does it concern?'

'I don't know the exact wording on your sheet, your Honour, but there's been a lot of talk in the provinces about a loss of identity.'

'Exactly what it says here; 'Charge Two – that the defendant has *Undermined the Provinces' Sense of Identity*.' Good; you can speak on this one.'

Thims cleared his throat, looked very grave, and began his speech.

'Honoured Listener and Honourable Representatives, this issue of *identity* has been the most distressing aspect for our people. The four provinces have always been at the heart of our existence, right back to our historic beginnings, the Great Divergence itself.' There was a low murmur of support from many PRs.

Thims looked around. He grew more confident – and more agitated. 'These *four* provinces are a cherished part of our nature, our purpose in this world. Deep down we may be *one* people, but we are *four* provinces. Valuable ancestral traditions have been simply swept away, consigned to the dustbin of history!' His voice lifted to a shout. 'Where, I ask you, is our glorious *heritage*?' He was reaching a dramatic finale, his arms waving madly and his eyes fixing his spellbound audience. 'We already had *unity*. What we don't want, is *uniformity*!'

Loud cries of approval greeted his last words, and he sat down, exhausted by the emotional effort involved. PRs patted him on the back. The Listener looked around for further comments, and the room quietened down. A single hand went up from the Elysian quarter. She stared in its direction and nodded. The lady PR was instantly recognisable as Sherdroc, the famous historian.

'This might not be the time to ask, but my friend's son Wesek, who wants to be an actor, is very keen on turning professional on the Cascadian 'Skim-Board.' Are you saying that this would not be permissible?'

'Correct! No chance whatsoever!' thundered the Listener.

'Skim-Boards for the Cascadians!' shouted the Cascadians.

'No Skim-Boards in Elysium!' replied the Elysians just as loudly.

'I'll take that as a 'no' then,' said Sherdroc politely.

Charge Three was read out, and a Grecian PR, Warlek, outlined the problem. 'This is a straightforward matter; *provincial security*. The frontiers used to be firm, but nowadays, our forces are dispersed. Great gaps have appeared in our lines of defence, morale amongst the troops is low, and it is only a matter of time before outsiders penetrate. I suggest that the recent formation of a Defence Force to cover all the provinces has been an unmitigated strategic *disaster.*'

'General Thorclan, this is a very serious accusation. Is this apparent sorry state of affairs true?' The question from the Listener was grave. The nervous Thorclan rose unsteadily to his feet; the mood of the meeting was getting to him. 'It's not *quite* that bad, Honourable Madam . . . er . . . your most worshipfulness. The assembled company must recall the recent Golf War – a notable success, and a tribute to the expertise and spirit of the troops. Indeed, you bestowed on me the honour of GLOB for my strong leadership.'

Vingal suddenly was looking ruffled. It was obvious that she had some sympathy with the old General. They had been on missions together, and she didn't really enjoy seeing the old soldier subjected to this treatment.

Warlek, however, didn't share these feelings of loyalty. 'Madam Listener, the Golf War proves my point. Why was it necessary? Because those MiGs had got past our defences! We shouldn't be fighting battles *inside* our own territory – the invaders should be stopped at the frontiers – but the frontiers are not defended. We're wide open!' There was strong support for this opinion with plenty of nods and shaking of heads, even from some Grecians. The longer distances they had been covering recently hadn't been popular with all the troops.

The Listener looked Thorclan full in the face. 'General, we need an honest answer to my next question. Please think carefully. Do you have *any* evidence that our defences have been breached by outsiders, or can we feel safe in your hands?'

General Thorclan visibly winced. He was only too aware of the smelly but well-spoken human stranger. He hesitated. His mouth was trying to form the right words.

Warlek pounced triumphantly. '*There* you are! He knows it's true, we're totally exposed! We should put up a sign saying, *Visitors welcome!*'

As the Assembly continued, matters didn't get any better from Jamie and Nigriff's point of view. It was incredible what was coming to light.

There was one charge about *Introducing Devastating*

Weapons of Warfare, which Jamie realised probably meant his crossbow.

There was even a charge of *Contacting Mysterious and Supernatural Energies*. The detail wasn't clear, but Jamie reckoned they were probably referring to the Pebble Alcove. By this point, he had sunk to the floor upstairs, and was staring through the banisters, gripping them tightly, hardly believing events. Nigriff was sat cross-legged, his head in his hands.

'The final charge is perhaps the most serious. It reads; "That the presence of a Mr. J. Thompson in Malplaquet has so *Destabilised the Existence of its True Inhabitants, that they are becoming Entirely Visible to Any and All Humans.*' "

She stopped to let the words sink in. Nigriff looked horrified, and swivelled round to see Jamie's reaction. Jamie was genuinely shocked. This was totally unexpected, it couldn't be true. What *had* he done? He was meant to be their protector, their Guide. Some of the mothers on the gallery put their arms around their children, and drew them closer.

The awful incident of the young girl and the slumbering Kasuya was outlined, the whole room hushed and attentive. The story concluded. 'Thus, I am afraid to say, that *not only* have we lost some of our precious heritage; *not only* have we lost our sense of unity; *not only* have we lost military security; we appear to have lost the *greatest* protection we ever had – being invisible to almost all members of the human race.'

There was a stunned silence, only broken by the sound of weeping from a woman upstairs. Through her sobs came her loud lament, 'What's to become of us – and our children?' The PRs shook their heads, one or two brandished their fists at Jamie, and Nigriff seemed very much alone. Only Thorclan, sat next to him, was offering any support, an arm around the hunched Librarian's shoulders.

'Can we vote now?' shouted one PR.

'Yes, the vote!' came the cry from others. 'We must have the vote!'

To her credit, the Listener resisted the shouts of the mob.

'Let me remind you,' she shouted above the din, 'that this is a courtroom, and not a normal Assembly. We *will* conduct our affairs with decorum.' She looked at the sad figure of Nigriff. 'Our learned friend has a right to reply.'

Nigriff raised his head. To the astonishment of those sat near him, his eyes were wet with tears.

'He's been crying,' whispered one woman, Lareck by name.

'Doesn't usually show any emotion,' said another.

'Shh !' said a third. 'He's about to speak; give him a chance.'

'Elysian Friends, Grecians, and other countrymen,' croaked Nigriff, as he was helped to his feet by Thorclan, 'this is a sad day. It has been deeply upsetting to hear the dismal condition of our beloved land. I can only apologise for my part in the affair. As honourable men and women, you deserve an explanation. Be assured, I am not here to praise the accused. Nevertheless,' and here he paused for effect, scanning their faces, 'I have here a copy of a document that promises his help to you and all your descendants.'

He had their attention.

'What is it, his will?' shouted out one PR.

'Quiet!' joined in another. 'Let Nigriff speak! What is this document?'

'I hardly dare read it,' replied Nigriff. 'It will stir up such strong feelings in you. It may be better for you not to know.'

'Read it!' came the cry. 'Read it out! Show it to us!'

Nigriff slowly put his hand inside his jacket and drew out a small piece of paper. He unfolded it carefully. Every eye was on him. He cleared his throat to speak.

'It's a poem. A poem about this person whose character has been assassinated. With your permission, I will read it.' He took the silence as their agreement.

He held the paper at arm's length and began.

> A Child no more, the Man appears,
> He comes of Age, the Hope of Years.
> Our Fount of Wisdom, whose Way is Delight
> True Source of all Pure Knowledge and Insight,
> Our Guide. . . .

His words were drowned by the reaction of the crowd.

'It's rubbish!' came one angry voice.

'Don't understand it!'

'It doesn't mean anything, Nigriff!'

The Listener held up her hand to quell the noise. Nigriff was stunned. This should have convinced the mob – it was genuine eighteenth-century poetry after all. Jamie caught his eye, and shrugged his shoulders as if to say, 'Nice try.'

Events moved rapidly to the vote – the inevitable vote against all that Jamie and Nigriff had been working to achieve. On the rug, only Thorclan (to his great credit) gave his support. After a very brief consultation with four advisers (Jamie had the feeling that it had all been decided beforehand anyway), the lady with the final authority composed herself to announce the verdict.

'Nigriff the Elysian, Senior Imperial Archivist, and also Chief Historian and Most Notable Librarian, step forward.' He did so. 'As a consequence of your actions in befriending this human outsider, you have brought the inhabitants of Malplaquet into the *gravest* danger. The fragile balance of nature has been upset. I have no alternative but to deprive you of your rank and titles. Please approach the bench. I instruct you to hand over, without further ado, your badge of office – the Golden Card of the Imperial Archives and Library.'

Nigriff stumbled forward and, with shaking hands, transferred the highly-prized item.

She held it up high in the air in both hands, grasping it tightly, and then with one wrench, tore it in half, and threw both pieces to the ground.

Nigriff groaned and sank to the floor. Thorclan rushed to his aid. Jamie wanted to run downstairs, but sensed it would only make matters worse. The Listener was also looking up sternly in his direction, so he assumed it was his verdict next.

'Young man,' she shouted, 'you are familiar to us as a special friend of the respected Granny. Many of us have lived in and cared about these gardens for many moons, and it is therefore time to be frank. Thompson, you have meddled in matters *far* beyond your merely human knowledge; you can see the widespread distress that your interference has caused. Severe steps have had to be taken to deal with the *former* Archivist, Nigriff; but let me assure you, that I took no pleasure in treating a respected colleague in such a way. As regards *your* penalty, there is a difficulty over your size. Nevertheless, we have found an answer; I have decided. . . .'

She never finished the sentence. Suddenly, the outside door burst open and Vicky ran in, panting and visibly upset.

'Quick! I'm sorry – but it's Yenech! He's been captured! I need help!'

14: The Search for Yenech

Vicky's words brought everything to an immediate standstill. All faces turned to her. She composed herself, brushed back her straggling hair and blushed slightly.

'I'm sorry, I know it's a big meeting, but it's Yenech – he's gone!'

The Listener, not surprisingly, reacted first. 'Young lady, you are clearly in distress, and so your intrusion is forgiven. But this is not the first time that Yenech has been – how shall I put it? – not easy to find. Are you sure he's been captured?'

Vicky was becoming more upset, and her words came out in a rush. 'Yes, I was *there*, the Elysian Fields, we were walking past the Worthies, I'd gone on ahead, and looked back, and this man jumped out and grabbed him and ran off, and it was horrible and I didn't know what to do.' The tears began.

Nigriff spoke up. 'Miss Vicky, are you saying this man is an *Elysian*?'

'No, that's the point – he's a human, my size!'

Pandemonium broke out. The crowds on the upper level rushed towards the staircase, and startled PRs rapidly gathered up their documents and scampered off the rug to the exit, tiny sheets of paper fluttering around them. Loud shouts could be heard above the general frenzy;

'It's like Kasuya!'

'I knew this would happen!'

'We should never have trusted Thompson – this is the end!'

'Captured by humans . . . never safe again!'

The Listener, with an almighty effort, raised her sharp voice above the din. 'QUIET! We do *not* behave like this! Stand where you are!' There was a pause. Her words still carried authority, even in times of panic. 'We must decide on a course of action – this is an *extremely* serious incident.'

The people looked at each other. From the door came a confident response. 'Madam – sorry, but that's why I'm going home. My wife and kids are out there – I'm not hanging around just to talk about it.'

There were some general shouts of approval – 'Quite right!' and 'Well said, Threapitoc!' – and lots of pushing and shoving, and soon there was a swarm of tiny people rushing past Vicky and streaming down across the fields in every direction. A handful of older PRs went up to the Listener, standing forlornly behind her pile of books, and had a quiet word before shuffling off quickly in some embarrassment.

Within a few minutes, she was the only member left in the room – apart from Nigriff and Thorclan, who had been watching events unfold around them. The last spectators from upstairs were running out of the door. Jamie was standing by Vicky and talking quietly, trying to comfort her.

The Listener gathered up her papers. 'I hope you're satisfied,' she said, looking fiercely at each in turn. 'In the history of our people, this is a day to remember, or rather a day to forget. I should add another charge – *Destroying our Ancient Political Institutions*. But there's no-one left to vote on it, or on anything else for that matter.' She threw her cloak around her shoulders. 'I don't suppose we'll be meeting each other here again. Goodbye.' And she strode out, dignified and proper to the last.

Thorclan spoke up. 'Miss Vicky, was this human the one we saw recently, that scoundrel with the long dark coat and large book?'

Vicky nodded glumly. Jamie looked surprised. Nigriff was

intrigued. 'A dark coat? Did he seem . . . untrustworthy?'

It was Thorclan's turn to nod in agreement.

'Was there anything else unusual about him?' continued Nigriff.

'He was really slimy and smelly,' sniffed Vicky.

'That's the man, the very same. I saw him a while ago, near the Rotunda, acting suspiciously. The esteemed Granny and I discussed him and, um . . .' Nigriff hesitated, remembering her opinion but not wanting to criticise the old lady, '. . . we felt that we lacked adequate information. We never saw him again.'

'But it sounds like he's been here all the time, waiting for his moment to strike,' mused Thorclan. 'Fooled me. I thought he was a dead loss – no backbone.'

'Right, we have to do something,' said Jamie. 'This isn't helping Yenech. Vicky – shoot back to Granny's and tell her what's happened. We'll see you there in ten minutes. Thorclan, Nigriff, come with me – we'll go through Elysium.'

He bent down to pick up the two small people. As he did so, he noticed two more standing by the door. He recognised them as Wesel and Hyroc. 'Hi fellas,' he said, in genuine surprise. 'What are you doing here? Haven't you both got homes to go to?'

They looked down, shifting from one foot to the other. Wesel spoke. 'Yes, sir, well, I mean, no sir. It's just that, well, we want to help.'

Hyroc joined in. 'We don't know about the charges and everything, sir, but we do know one thing. That Cold Stream Cup was the best thing we've ever done, and Yenech was in our team, sir, and we want to find him.'

Jamie and the others were deeply moved by their words. Nigriff went over and actually hugged Hyroc. Thorclan shook Wesel's hand, muttering, 'Good show.' Vicky burst into tears again.

'Brilliant,' enthused Jamie. 'Just like the good old days – the Thompson Quad Squad back in action! Right, you two go with Vicky, and we'll see you soon.' He lifted up Nigriff and placed him carefully in his inside jacket pocket, closely followed by Thorclan.

'More undercover work?' asked the old soldier, poking his head out.

'Afraid so,' replied Jamie. 'Neither of you are welcome in Elysium anymore – nor am I, to be honest.' He closed the door of the Gothic Temple and strode off down the hill.

As Jamie gingerly clambered over the stile behind the Worthies, he heard his two companions chattering away.

'The villain could be anywhere, Nigriff.'

'I suspect Master Jamie has a plan.'

'Just like his Gratton campaign. Back-up's a bit light though.'

'One needs brains as well as brawn, General.'

'You never spoke a truer word, Nigriff, never. . . .'

'Shh, you two!' hissed Jamie. 'No noise!' He trod gingerly over the damp and slippery planks of the Shell Bridge and headed up the slope to the Temple of Ancient Virtue. Everywhere was still, as if all living things had gone to ground. Once inside the Temple, Jamie stopped in the very centre of the circular room, deliberately soaking up its atmosphere. He cast his eyes over the statues of four famous Greeks. Then came Thorclan's exclamation, followed by Nigriff's reply.

'Eureka!'

'I beg your pardon, but I am sure that I do not.'

'No, not you – the smell!'

'I understood you perfectly well the first time – but there are two of us in here, and thus it is extremely cramped, and it has been difficult recently to attend to one's personal hygiene. . . .' The two of them carried on wittering away, Thorclan trying to explain the misunderstanding, and Nigriff trying to justify his washing habits.

'Good,' thought Jamie, listening closely to their conversation, 'as I expected.' He bent his head down and whispered, 'Hold tight, I'm going to run to Granny's.' He bounced down the steps, to the sound of muffled groans and occasional grunts from his jacket pocket.

At Granny's, Vicky had calmed down with a cup of tea, and the two of them were chatting quietly together. Wesel and Hyroc were happily struggling with lumps of Brownie cake. Jamie kissed the old lady, said a few words of reassurance, and prised out his tiny luggage and placed them on the table. They seemed relieved to be back on something solid.

'Over to you, General,' he said. 'What can you tell us?'

'It was the smell, you know – very distinctive.'

Nigriff opened his mouth to speak but Jamie signalled to him to be quiet. 'In what way?' 'On the northeast frontier; Vicky and I met him. I was in her bag, and his stench was strangely familiar, a mixture; damp clothes, stale food, unwashed body, foul breath, the odour of mud and stagnant water. There's only one thing in the whole world smells like that; a soldier living rough. The man's under canvas.'

Nigriff was relieved to hear the explanation for the smell – and also impressed. 'Good reasoning, General. The Elysian air has done you some good.'

Jamie interrupted. 'Not the *air*, Nigriff – remember? Anyway,' he continued, 'we reckon he's living in some woods, and probably nearby to keep an eye on us. Any ideas where?'

Various possibilities came up – the thick belt of trees around the Bourbon Fields, the woods to the west of the Queen's Temple, the thick shrubbery to the south of the Eleven-Acre Lake. These were all rejected because of the roving presence of the Grecian army, who would undoubtedly have spotted his camp in any of these hideouts.

Granny offered an interesting suggestion; the Japanese Gardens. Her arguments were that the area was incredibly overgrown, very local but 'Off the beaten track', and because it belonged to no particular province, it wasn't watched that carefully. Finally, she declared, 'He could have been looking for some past evidence.'

'Like the model city,' added Jamie.

'Precisely,' she replied.

It was hard to disagree with her reasoning. Thorclan took control. 'I'll get the squirrels on to it straightaway. Can't ask them to cover all of Malplaquet, but if we've narrowed it down to that sector, then we're in with a chance. Leave it to me,' he said gruffly, and shot out of the door, ready to hail the next passing rodent.

'And now,' said Jamie, 'we'll make our rescue plans.'

Thorclan's reconnaissance on the back of a squirrel did confirm Granny's brilliant combination of logic and guesswork. Deep in the innermost recesses of the Japanese Gardens, far away from prying eyes, he spotted a well-camouflaged shelter of sticks, branches and muddy green tarpaulin, built over one of the old sunken paths. Thorclan even saw the kidnapper creep out at one stage, just to break off a few leafy branches from a nearby tree.

'At least he's changing his bed,' the General acknowledged on his return. 'Must have had some army training.'

As dusk settled that evening, 'Operation Happy Camper' swung into action. Anybody watching (and who knows, there might have been a tiny person or two snatching a quick peek) would have seen a small gaggle of people stealthily making their way past Friendship to the Palladian Bridge.

Jamie was in front with a rucksack across his shoulders, closely followed by Vicky in her long coat, and then Granny shuffling along at the back. Her attire was unusual; heavy boots, patched dirty trousers, a torn and tatty duffel coat, a couple of colourful but faded scarves scrunched about her neck, and a battered pot-shaped hat.

If the light had been better, one might have noticed four small figures peering out of various pockets, whispering and exchanging hand signals.

The mood of the whole party was sombre but purposeful; they had a job to do.

Squeezing their way through the gate that led past the Chinese House, they lightly tip-toed down the steps to the Cascade, relieved that the noise of the splashing waterfall covered their movements. They entered the Japanese Gardens via the old wooden gate between two high banks.

Nigriff yanked Jamie's coat hard, and motioned to him to bend down.

'Master Jamie, this is *such* a historic place. We must avoid damaging it. Did you know, for example, that in this very spot, the great Snilloc himself, he of the mighty right arm, once despatched four. . . .'

'Nigriff,' whispered Jamie in some consternation, 'this isn't the best time for a history lesson. Tell us later – Yenech can hear the story then as well.'

Nigriff got the point. 'Yes, sir, I see what you mean, sir. And this is where you want me to stay, isn't it, sir?'

Jamie nodded, gently placed him on the ground by a moss-covered stone, waved farewell, and the team continued on their way.

Fifty metres on, barely visible in the gloom and very foreboding and grim, was the hideaway of Yenech's captor. Jamie sensed Vicky shudder. He wasn't feeling that brave himself, but they had made their plans, learnt their particular parts, and checked and re-checked the details. Thorclan himself had declared that if it came off – or rather, *when* it came off – medals would be awarded, and the campaign would be remembered with an annual dinner.

But that was in the future. In the present, they had to put the plan into action.

They edged forward until they were lying on the slight rise of a bank, less than ten metres from the tent. They could hear movement inside, and see torchlight drifting across the fabric. Then they heard his voice in conversation, and panicked at the idea of two kidnappers, until they realised he was on the phone. His posh voice, even hushed, was familiar to Vicky and Thorclan, who exchanged knowing glances.

'*Terrific* news, sir, a male, but probably not grade 1 . . . one does one's best, sir . . . jolly hard to find the little blighters . . . of course, a female next . . . yes, sir, good breeding . . . quality people . . . eight o'clock in the morning . . . and the, er, little matter of money? Hello? Hello? Dash it, phone's run out. . . .'

There was muttering, fortunately not too clear, and then it was quiet again.

'As we thought,' whispered Jamie. 'Under orders to get another one.'

Vicky disagreed. 'Not another *one* – but *lots*. Don't you see? A male and female – this is the start of a breeding programme. Poor Yenech!'

Jamie realised this was an awful prospect, and that the little chap simply had to escape. He signalled to Granny, who crawled over, puffing and groaning slightly.

'Not much fun at my age,' she muttered, 'but Yenech does need us.'

'Definitely,' agreed Jamie. 'You're okay about seeing this man?'

'Absolutely,' said Granny positively. 'Even if he'd met me, he'll never recognise me with all this mud on my face. Organic cosmetics. Here we go.'

Quietly she heaved herself up, slid down the bank and stepped gingerly towards the tent-flap. Before the owner realised, she was halfway in and gushing. 'A very good evening to you. Goodness me, what a palaver! I never thought we'd end up here after Newbury! Gardens like these, nothing's sacred these days.'

In the silence of the woods, those hiding on the bank could hear most of the conversation. Granny was doing her stuff splendidly. 'I am correct, aren't I? You were there, at Solsbury Hill? I'm sure I know you. Allow me to introduce myself. Lucinda – but you can call me Boggy, all my best friends do.'

'I'm most awfully sorry, but your face isn't familiar and you're horribly dirty. I'm going to have to ask you to leave.' His tone was emphatic.

Granny stuck to her task. 'But aren't you protesting? About the by-pass? The Dadford-Chackmore Link, you know, the final section of the M25?'

'Madam, this is most unfortunate, but you are mistaken. I live here.'

'And that's your hamster, is it? How sweet! Could I possibly see him?'

'Certainly not! Now I really must insist, I don't wish to resort to violence. . . .'

'Alright, don't get your knickers in a twist!' Granny emerged in a hurry through the canvas opening. 'Remember me to Squelchy!' she shouted over her shoulder. She adjusted her hat, smoothed her coat, and sauntered over to the team patiently waiting and lying hidden.

'*Such* a nice man,' she whispered calmly. 'Yenech is there, in a plastic hamster cage – a round one. In his combats, curled up in some leaves, fast asleep.'

Before the owner realised, Granny was halfway in.

'Aaah,' soothed Vicky. 'At least he's safe.'

'Not yet,' said Jamie, 'but soon. Phase two. Vicky, Hyroc? You next. Wesel, get cracking on the cage. General – check the cavalry.'

Jamie emptied some items from his rucksack and handed the bag to Vicky, who popped Hyroc inside, pulled the string tight at the top, slung it over her shoulder, and then picked her way silently over to the tent. It was becoming quite murky by now, so she shone her torch on the ground in front. Wesel and Thorclan slipped off into the gloom.

Jamie and Granny shuffled closer. 'Timing's everything,' whispered Jamie.

'And acting,' replied Granny. Then they heard Vicky's voice. 'Hello, excuse me – anybody in?' She was bending down by the entrance.

'Brave girl,' thought Jamie. 'She loathes the man.'

'Oh my word, not another!' was the initial angry response. A head and shoulders poked out of the canvas, and a torch flashed on her face. 'Well, hello,' came his smooth voice trying to ooze charm, as he saw Vicky smiling sweetly at him. 'Can I help you?'

'Yes, hello. I just bumped into an old lady; she said you were living here.'

'Indeed I am,' said the head.

'Well, I so enjoyed our conversation the other day, you know, talking about little things you can discover in these gardens, and I found this today.' Vicky loosened the cord at the top of the bag. 'Can I show you it – or rather, *him*?'

That final word catapulted him forward. 'Now that sounds jolly interesting.' He shone his torch inside the rucksack. At the bottom lay Hyroc, cowering in one corner and shielding his eyes from the light. The man was impressed. 'My word! Where did you find this little fellow?'

Jamie heard Vicky explaining that she had stumbled across a small nest of them not far away. She claimed that most of them had fled, but she'd captured another one in a cage 'by that big tree round the corner.'

'It wouldn't be a female, I mean, a *lady* by any chance?' came the swift question.

'I'm not sure, it's hard to tell when they're so little, but it might be.' In an instant he was following her away from the tent.

As soon as Jamie thought it was safe, he and Granny crept round to the back of the canvas shelter and slipped under the covering. Their work was swift but successful. Yenech was woken from his slumbers, and a toy soldier about the same size, dressed in combats, was bent into position to replace him. Granny and Yenech made good their escape, heading swiftly and silently back to the Cascade, while Jamie hung around in the dark shadows to watch what happened.

Vicky and her companion had arrived at the tree, at the base of which her torch revealed a tiny figure, trapped inside a cage made of intertwined roots and branches. It was Wesel, standing with his hands against the bars, looking very frightened.

'Not bad,' thought Vicky to herself. 'How did he manage to get himself stuck in his own design?' (She didn't know he'd had years of practice).

'Oh, look, it is a male,' she said. 'An easy mistake with this one.'

Wesel gave her a fierce stare. The kidnapper grunted unhappily under his breath.

'Let's have a closer look, shall we?' said Vicky, bending down towards the cage. At this precise moment she suddenly caught her foot in a root, or so it seemed, and stumbled forward, knocking into the man and Wesel's prison.

It collapsed like a pack of cards, precisely as it was designed to do. The rucksack fell off her shoulder, and a small group of squirrels shot across the area – only pausing long enough for two tiny figures to leap on their backs. One of the rodents was carrying a General.

In the panic Vicky jumped to her feet, hid behind a large bush, shouted out, 'Sorry, I think it's escaped!' and ran off through the undergrowth. The man tried to find his torch (which had been kicked out of the way), and groped his way around in the dark. 'Look, this isn't funny, it's a real nuisance. Where are you?'

Hearing and seeing nothing in the gloom, he turned round in a frenzy and attempted to hurry back to his squalid home, which involved lots of scratching and bumping and bruising – and far too much bad language. Close to his den, his feet suddenly came into contact with a solid lump of something, and he sprawled headlong over a stone sculpture of a small lion that he couldn't remember ever having seen there before.

From the safety of a nearby bush, Vicky watched and listened to his frantic struggles; she hoped she had given the others enough time. Soon she heard a match being struck inside the tent, and thought it might have been followed by a sigh of relief. Did that mean that Yenech was still in the cage? Vicky had no way of knowing whether the whole rescue had worked properly or not.

She quickly met up with Jamie, who told her the good news about Yenech, and the two of them made their way silently back to the Cascade. There they found a proud Grecian General, a successful Palladian builder (or 'creative architect'), and a Cascadian escape-artist, all on squirrel-back. Also present were Nigriff and Granny . . . and resting in her arms was Yenech.

He was bleary-eyed and a bit confused, but obviously happy.

'It's not that bad, being a hamster, you know,' he said cheerfully. 'Mind you, he never did set up one of those nice water-bottles for me.'

Vicky stroked him. 'Do you think hamsters enjoy this?' she asked.

'*Definitely*,' he purred. 'Very nice.'

'You have been extremely fortuitous, Yenech,' said Nigriff. 'We found out that you were to be the key person in an extensive new breeding programme.'

'I see,' replied Yenech thoughtfully. 'So that was a lucky escape, wasn't it?'

15: Conflict on the Lakes

Back at Granny's the celebrations were in full swing. 'Hamsters do have it easy,' said Yenech, 'but thanks for coming to get me anyway.' He was especially grateful to Wesel and Hyroc for their loyalty. 'I would have been lost without you, you know.'

'Er, ye-es, probably,' agreed Wesel.

As they all sat around, they re-lived the superb rescue; Granny as a road protester, Vicky's bravery in talking to the man again, Hyroc the 'captive' in the bag, Wesel's brilliant self-collapsing cage, Thorclan's squirrel cavalry, and the daring snatch of Yenech by Granny and Jamie.

Nigriff was happy just to listen to the tales, although one question was still bothering him. 'What will he do when he discovers that his captive has been replaced by a toy?'

'There you are, Yenech,' roared Thorclan, with a huge guffaw, 'I knew you'd turn into a model soldier one day!' The ex-hamster took the joke well, but still had concerns. 'Did you say he was handing me – and a female – over at eight o'clock tomorrow morning? And that he would get paid?'

Vicky nodded. 'Yes – but that won't be happening.'

'But surely he'll be upset?'

'Furious,' added Granny. 'If he's any sense, he won't bother turning up.'

That was the problem – *did* the villain have any sense? And what about the person expecting to collect two small packages?

Early next morning, with bodies gently snoozing around the cottage on spare pillows and mattresses, Granny was the first up. Crumbs of cake and biscuits were littering the table after the small party, so she swept them into the front of her apron. 'Special treat for the ducks,' she thought.

She ambled round to the Octagon Lake, and gazed across the water for any signs of wildlife. The lake had nobody on it, but beyond the Cascade she glimpsed movement amongst the trees on the far bank. She stared hard in that direction – and let drop all the crumbs. It wasn't a duck, but a person – and not just *any* person.

'My word!' she exclaimed. 'He's not given up!' She bustled back to the cottage and raised the alarm. 'Jamie! Vicky! He's out there – across the Eleven-Acre!'

They were outside in an instant, laces flapping on their trainers and Jamie struggling with his sleeves. Dashing over to the Cascade, they shaded their eyes to look across the glistening water. It had been foolish to think their opponent would give up, especially after being tricked. But there was no sign of life. He'd already moved on.

'I bet he's heading towards Venus,' panted Vicky. 'Come on, we can get there first.' They sprinted off, scattering rabbits, and eyes scanning the woodland.

'If we've lost him, we're in trouble,' puffed Jamie. 'He'll be after Cascadians!'

Before long, absolutely breathless, they stopped in front of the old Temple. No person of any size whatsoever was to be seen. Jamie knew that sometimes Cascadians did go for an early-morning row on the lake, but they were probably lying low after yesterday's big scare. The only movement of any sort was the door of the boat-hut on its island.

It was swinging gently on its hinges.

Jamie and Vicky looked at each other, both thinking the same thing. 'The safety-boat!' gasped Jamie. An inflatable dinghy with a powerful outboard motor, teachers used it to assist pupils who got into difficulties learning to sail. It was ideal for rescuing boys – and doubtless also for outrunning smaller people in boats.

'Quick – follow me!' urged Jamie, setting off with renewed

energy. In less than a minute they were racing across the narrow footbridge to the island, and were pleased to see the boat ahead of them still leaning against the hut. 'It must have been left outside,' said Vicky hopefully, crossing the bridge behind Jamie. 'Don't know,' he replied. 'We'll check anyway.'

Vicky didn't want to meet the man again. 'Not so fast,' she said, 'keep together.'

Water was gently lapping against the old wooden landing-platform as they pushed past overgrown bushes to the hut. One of its two green doors was open. They peered in. Through the gloom they made out the blue sailing dinghies, and canoes stacked up against the far wall. Life jackets were hanging up on rusty brackets, and there was a smell of diesel.

Jamie carefully walked in to get a closer look, Vicky staying in the doorway. He asked her to move as she was blocking the light, so she stepped forward. As she did so, the door suddenly slammed shut and they were in almost total darkness. There was the sound of a padlock being snapped across the bolt outside, and then came a familiar voice.

'Neat, very neat, rats in a trap. The little mice next. . . .'

Jamie ran at the door, but caught his foot in some ropes and sprawled headlong. Picking himself up, he hammered against the door with his fists, but it was locked solid. There was no way out. And there was no point in shouting at that time of day, especially against the new sound of an outboard motor being revved up.

'Blast!' he moaned. 'How stupid! Come on, we've got to get out.'

Much was happening at Granny's. She had roused the others and was getting the GT out of the shed. Thorclan was insisting that someone should go with her. 'Madam, this is very brave of you, but you should *not* undertake this mission alone.'

'General, I'm sorry, but this is too dangerous. He might be armed, and it's your lot that he's after. Stay here and keep out of sight.' She turned the ignition, the engine burst into life with a mighty purr, and she chugged off towards the lake.

Nigriff shook his head. 'We must keep an eye on events,' he advised the others. So the five of them – Nigriff and Thorclan, along with Yenech, Hyroc and Wesel – took up position in one of the Lake Pavilions. Its raised platform gave a good open view over both the lakes and the nearby paths.

In a grim mood, Granny drove down to the Eleven-Acre, looking carefully around her en route. The furthest banks, by the boating island, were covered with thick bushes and shrubs, and they made it hard to see what was happening. To her relief, there were no other signs of life – apart from two Cascadians getting into their special Single-Sail boats. She recognised one as Tuckted, the Inter-Provincial Games champion, and she thought the other might be Cirep, a cousin of Cyrep. There was no time for casual greetings.

'The intruder's here!' she gabbled. 'Get out of the water!'

'Thanks for the warning, Madam – I believe the safest place is *on* the water,' replied Tuckted confidently. 'Right, Cirep, this morning's lesson has now become Speed and Manoeuvre. When you're ready.' They made final adjustments to the rigging and the sails, caught the slight offshore breeze, and both boats glided away. Granny pushed hard on her accelerator and moved off. 'That was lucky,' she thought. 'But where have Vicky and Jamie gone?' The GT trundled on, the high-pitched whine of its straining engine drowning the distant sound of an outboard motor by the boat-hut.

The two captives had been looking through some cracks in the hut's panels.

'The GT's stopped by the bank,' said Jamie anxiously. 'I don't know why.'

'If she comes round here, we'll be okay. Keep shouting,' said Vicky. They continued banging on the walls and trying to make their voices heard. But the safety boat's engine was roaring, powering the craft in a straight line across the water.

'He's after something,' gasped Vicky, desperately peering through the small gap.

'Some*one*,' corrected Jamie sadly. 'We *must* get out. . . . Jam that oar in the doors.'

Despite years of practice and his undoubted skill, Tuckted never stood a chance. Cirep was the first to be snatched. She was sailing along, just starting to get the hang of it, when suddenly her boat was lifted out of the water. She herself was grabbed and squashed inside a round plastic cage that contained leaves and a toy soldier. Her craft was snapped in half and flung back overboard.

Tuckted put up more of a fight, using all his expertise to flee from his pursuer. There was a frantic gibing, tacking, beating into the wind, luffing and even screaming, before he too was hauled out of the water and his precious boat was cracked in two. Inside the hamster cage he beat his fists against the clear wall, and shouted up at the scruffy and grinning figure, 'My friends will get you for that!'

'Gosh, I am petrified,' came the sneering reply from a huge ugly face pressed close. 'Perhaps your children will help. You'll have hundreds soon!' He pulled out a silver watch. 'Awfully good timing; nearly eight o'clock.' He yanked the lever on the outboard, and the craft lifted its nose and sped towards the higher Octagon Lake.

Granny had just emerged from trees by Venus when she heard the motor, and had seen the entire episode. She felt helpless and responsible. 'This is getting worse and worse,' she groaned, watching the boat head to the outer limits of Cascadia. 'Jamie, Vicky – where are you?'

Her question was answered by a loud '*crack*!' as the boat-hut doors crashed open. Her two young friends spilled out and shouted across. 'Granny, go back your side – we'll head him off this way!' They disappeared round the back of the hut to the footbridge.

Time was not on their side. Before they had gone far, the boat with its three occupants had reached the Cascade, and the driver had jumped onto the bank and was starting to drag the boat out of water and up the grassy slope to the upper lake. Once on the Octagon he would get even further ahead.

The Quad Squad and their latest recruit had watched the unfolding events with alarm. Two of their people had been kidnapped, and three adults had been unable to prevent it.

'It's grim,' muttered Thorclan from behind a pillar. 'If those three can't do it. . . .'

'Then the Thompson Quad Squad can,' insisted Yenech. 'We're at our best with the odds against us. I've an idea – follow me!' He slid down over the top step.

Nigriff looked at the General, unhappy at the idea of following Yenech at *any* time, especially now. 'Desperate times, desperate measures, General.' 'Desperate is the word, Nigriff,' he agreed. Yenech was already at the bottom of the flight of steps and was heading off in a direction away from the Cascade, and towards the Pebble Alcove.

'That *can't* be the right way,' Thorclan muttered, watching his driver sprint off into the distance. 'Why am I not surprised?' Then to his shock he saw, on the far skyline by an avenue of Cypress trees, a black car easing its way along the track. 'Good grief, the pick-up! Move yourself, Thorclan – still time for one last fight.' He quickly lowered himself down the steps and hurried after the scurrying Yenech. All he could hear was the rapid thumping of his heart, his own hard breathing – and the splash of a boat being slipped into the water near the top of the Cascade.

'Jamie, its too late, the boat's in the top lake – and I've a terrible stitch!' Vicky was struggling to keep up with Jamie, who in spite of his fall in the hut was leaping his way through the woods. On the other bank he spotted the GT, ambling along at top speed, and unlikely to get there in time. 'We've got to keep going!' shouted Jamie behind him. He knew their chances were slim, but he hadn't heard the boat's motor start up yet.

Granny had her foot hard to the floor, secretly cursing the restricted power of the buggy. 'One day,' she was thinking, 'I'll get this upgraded. Come *on!*' She rounded the final corner by the rough stonework arch of the Cascade, and saw the boat next to the bank. The kidnapper was hunched over the outboard, yanking the cord, breathing heavily and looking towards the Gothic Temple and the car cruising slowly past it. Granny decided she had no choice but to drive straight at the boat.

The man lifted his head with a look that was a mixture of sheer disbelief and genuine amusement. An old lady in an overgrown golf-trolley was about to ram his speedboat.

One more pull, the engine caught, and the boat surged away just as the GT shambled over the edge.

At that very same moment, Jamie came hurtling round his final bend, and saw everything. The boat powered off, the driver shouted something rude back at the trolley-owner, and the front of her beloved vehicle dipped into the water with an apologetic splash and sizzle, closely followed by a cloud of steam as a finale.

Granny was never in any real danger – the water was so shallow that it only half-covered the front wheels – but she was fuming as Jamie helped her out.

'Nasty man! What a cheek – women drivers indeed!' She stood there forlornly looking at the waterlogged GT, and at the safety-boat speeding away.

Vicky joined them at the water's edge. She put her arm round Granny. The black car was inching its way down the hill towards the Palladian Bridge, the hand-over point. They could only watch. There was absolutely nothing they could do.

They had tried . . . and failed.

Yenech was busy giving orders. 'This is the narrowest part. He's bound to see us. General, stand there in the open. Wesel, pull back that branch, and string it up like I said.'

Thorclan was concerned about his very visible position, but Nigriff had persuaded him to trust Yenech. 'He has changed, General. His mental abilities have increased dramatically.'

'Not difficult, Nigriff,' was the reply. 'Last night he was happy being a hamster.'

Yenech was fully in charge. 'Hyroc, try to find two. They're round here somewhere.' The Cascadian darted off into the undergrowth. 'Wesel, hide in this long grass with me. General, stay out front and wave. Nigriff, only *exactly* when I say so.'

Very prominent, Thorclan stood on the bank as the boat approached the narrows. Was this Yenech's revenge, after years of rude comments about his sense of direction? The General contemplated retreat, but it wasn't an option for an old soldier – and anyway the boat was now drawing level with him. He could see the hard eyes of the dirty figure gripping the outboard's arm, staring directly ahead at the car by the bridge.

Thorclan waved nervously and gently. No response.

He waved both arms. Still nothing.

He jumped up and down, flapping his arms and shouting at the same time.

That did the trick. He'd been spotted.

The motor quietened to a steady purr, and the craft glided over. Thorclan heard the dreaded rounded vowels. 'Wonderful . . . splendid . . . another little chap. More pennies.'

A large grimy hand stretched out. Thorclan stood his ground, too scared now to move. The claw was drawing closer, fingers ready to tighten in a grip.

'Now!' shouted a voice from behind the General.

A springy '*swish*' of a branch, and a small volley of twigs flew at the human. Most fell short. A few bounced off him. The overall effect was predictably pathetic.

'So this one's got some chums, has it?'

'Not any more,' thought Thorclan, 'what on earth is Yenech up to?'

The human got down to ground level. 'Call that a bow?'

'No, *this* is a bow!' shouted Yenech, parting the long grass behind Thorclan, revealing Jamie's red crossbow, armed and ready, pointing directly at the human. Nigriff released the catch, and the dart with its black sucker slammed onto an expanse of dirty forehead.

The attack had the benefit more of surprise than force, causing the pilot to instinctively throw himself back into the boat, right against the throttle lever. As the craft immediately leapt forward, he lost his balance, banged his head hard on the engine casing, and lay there, motionless. The boat swirled round and headed back the way it had come, a massive wake spreading out behind.

TQS emerged from hiding and congratulated the relieved General. The black car did a tight turn and drove back up the hill. In the opposite direction the boat was still surging back to the Cascade, a scruffy figure slumped by the motor.

'It's coming this way!' shouted Vicky. They had been shocked to see, just a few minutes ago, the boat slowing to a halt by the bank and the man leaning across, and amazed when he had hurled himself backwards and revved the engine. Now it was at full throttle, probably heading in their direction – now *definitely* in their direction!

'Look out!' yelled Jamie. They threw themselves to the ground as the boat hit the low bank at top speed. Its raised prow bumped over the grassy edge, and then slid across the hard path, the wrecked propeller showering sparks en route.

The initial jolt caused a hamster cage to bounce out. Vicky swiftly picked it up and lifted the lid off, and fortunately the Lilliputian contents seemed dazed but intact. That same bump also woke up an adult male in the boat, who opened his eyes to see himself hurtling at tremendous speed straight through an eighteenth-century arch above a waterfall. It was like a Log Flume he had once been on. But this one had a three-metre, totally vertical drop. His scream was terrific and echoed around the lakes.

'Wicked!' enthused Jamie, as the boat flew out like a horizontal rocket, flipped over in mid-air, and deposited its human cargo in the lake with a spectacular splash.

For a brief moment it seemed as if the figure floating face down in the water had had his last (and possibly even first) good wash. And then without warning, he leapt up into the air with a piercing yell. A long silver-coloured object was thrashing about on his right hand. It was a huge fish, clamped to his fingers and making him extremely unhappy.

'Nasty. Looks like a Lenal,' said Granny.

'Or a Vazedir,' said Jamie. 'Very vicious.' The cleaned villain was jumping around in the shallows, cursing the flailing fish and trying to pull it off. Scrambling on to dry land still in a frenzy, a low branch caught him full across the forehead, and for the second time in ten minutes he was knocked out. The fish released its grip and slumped lifeless next to him.

Everything went quiet, just a few ripples lapping against the water's edge.

'I know,' said Jamie. 'Vicky, my bike padlock – quick!'

Visitors to Malplaquet later that day were pleased to find an authentic and deranged hermit chained up at the Hermitage. The National Trust had apparently not only provided them with a live exhibit, but had also kitted him out in proper hermit-style clothes.

'Takes *ages* to get that effect,' said one knowing father, standing amongst the crowds of onlookers outside the stone dwelling. 'You have to live in your clothes for weeks for that image – my teenage son's got it cracked.'

'Membership money well spent,' added another. 'Mind you, ranting and raving like that, he looks a complete nutter. I'm just glad he's tied up.'

Hidden in a nearby bush, Granny and Jamie were delighted. The hermit's garbled stories about tiny people living in the grounds were met with polite laughs and applause, especially his tale of these people shooting him, and sending him over the Cascade in a boat. Eventually, when a groundsman set him free with a fretsaw and began to roughly escort him off the premises, the old lady and her young friend were ready to breathe a huge sigh of relief.

Unfortunately his final words made that impossible. He lifted his head and shouted, so it seemed, to the whole gardens, 'You wait – Biddle will find out!'

Jamie was shocked. That name again – and no longer just a name in a history book, but like a real person. He noticed Granny shiver. 'That's *not* good news,' she said. 'We need to find Vicky and Nigriff. I don't like this one bit.'

Jamie knew what she meant. They were no longer fighting against a smelly character hiding in the woods. Somebody by the name of Biddle was around. This was much more serious – like those warnings of conflict in Pope's prophecy. Was this to do with Nigriff's *Forces of Restoration and Destruction*?

Perhaps this little ambush was only the start.

After many centuries, it sounded as if the real enemy had stirred again.

Biddle.

16: The End of the Beginning

'But what do we know about this Biddle person?' asked Vicky later, looking at the others in the room – especially Nigriff. After his previous collapse at the mere mention of the name, she was still wary of just dropping it into conversation.

'It's obviously not the original one after all this time,' volunteered Granny. 'Pity really – we'd easily sort out someone who's been collecting his pension for two hundred and fifty years.'

'He's got to be a descendant,' said Jamie. 'I bet it was him on the other end of the phone last night, and in the black car today. He's definitely after your people, Nigriff. Maybe the information has been in the family for generations.'

'Can we cope by ourselves?' asked Granny. 'This is serious stuff now.'

'We're not quite by ourselves,' replied Jamie. 'There's the Pebble Alcove.'

'Pebble *Archive*,' added Nigriff.

'Could be,' agreed Jamie. 'When it shows the Gulliver story, it helps us, gives us hints. I thought of chaining up Old Smelly after seeing Gulliver like it.'

'So it's guiding us . . .' mused Nigriff. 'A Pebble *Oracle* even. Fascinating.'

'And we know that other temples are affecting you all,' said Jamie. 'I tried it again yesterday with Thorclan at Ancient Virtue, and he recognised that smell straightaway. Inspiration.'

'Or *perspiration*,' corrected Thorclan, recalling the comments on body odour.

Jamie continued. 'Except I think I've worked something else out. It's not *all* the temples. Think about it – what did the prophecy say they were?' Vicky got it first. 'Restored?'

'Exactly. It's only the *repaired* buildings – like Venus or Ancient Virtue – that change people, not the ones that are still in a mess.'

'So the temples are *restored* . . . the people become more like each other, uniting . . .' said Granny, mulling over the idea.

'And let us not forget,' said Nigriff, 'that we also become *visible*. Remember Kasuya.'

'Bingo, that's brilliant!' exclaimed Jamie, his mind making connections fast. 'Of course! Fast asleep by Ancient Virtue, spotted by a little girl – it's the same thing. The people of Lilliput unite, the empire becomes strong – revealed – and so are the people. They start to appear. Like that line of Pope's – *the sea-people great appear.* It's all coming true!' He was flushed with excitement.

Granny was beaming. 'This is *wonderful*. I've waited years.' She hugged Vicky and Jamie.

Nigriff put a dampener on it. 'But this means that we can now be *seen*. Yet we cannot all hide on an island as before. How can we possibly live in safety?'

Granny wouldn't let her moment of delight be spoiled. 'There'll be an answer somehow, Nigriff. I suppose as long as you're careful near the restored buildings, it shouldn't be a problem.'

Something was still bothering Jamie. Why was it that the Lilliputians could now be spotted more easily? The prophecy said they would appear, but why should it be apparently caused by restored temples?

He thought about his own ability to see them – his *sensitivity,* as Granny called it. What was it she had once said? 'Not just the facts in the guidebooks, but feeling the place.' Most of the visitors only thought about its history. But now that the temples were being restored, it was making more humans aware of Malplaquet's special beauty and atmosphere. . . . In fact that was exactly it!

It wasn't just the Lilliputians being revealed.

It was also the humans becoming more sensitive.

Jamie explained. 'Loads of people are beginning to 'feel' what the garden's about, they can *sense* things they couldn't before. Restoring Malplaquet is making the *hidden* things appear. Amazing.'

Nigriff admired the logic, but he was also worried. 'Young Master, I do not doubt the *sense* in this, if that is the right word, but it is also most perplexing. The prophecy holds out great hope for us, the people of Lilliput, but we are now in greater danger than ever before.'

'But Nigriff, it fits your ideas about restoration and destruction,' said Jamie. 'It's exactly what's happening – things getting better and worse at the same time.' Nigriff pondered this, nodding thoughtfully.

'Is there anything else for you to do Jamie, you know, as the Guide?' asked Vicky. Granny was already half-way across to the cupboard. The ancient paper was once again spread out. This time their eyes alighted on one phrase that they hadn't paid much attention to before; *The Capital Gained.*

'The Capital? What's the capital round here?' asked Vicky.

Jamie offered a suggestion. 'I reckon it's got to be the mansion.'

'Why the mansion?' asked Vicky

'It's in the right place.' They all looked at him with puzzled expressions. 'I was looking at the map in Gulliver's Travels the other day,' explained Jamie. 'It's weird, but Lilliput and Malplaquet are similar shapes. And the mansion's built right where the capital Mildendo was.'

Vicky was the first to react. 'But the mansion's a school! How can you 'gain' that?' She was now finding this too much. 'Hang on; we can perhaps look after a few little people, but we can't take on 500 boys, never mind all the teachers.'

Granny joined in. 'I don't know about the shapes, Jamie, it's probably just a coincidence, but the mansion *is* the biggest building. It has to be the capital. There's obviously a job to be done – and only one way to do it.'

'Which is?' said Jamie, interested but apprehensive.

'You start school there this September.'

'*What!* You can't be serious?'

'Why not?'

'Lots of reasons – mainly money. Do you know what it costs to go there?'

'Almost to the penny. Your Father and I have often chatted about the school fees.'

'But there's no way that Dad can afford it.'

'No, but I can help – I've got a little put by for a rainy day.'

Jamie was excited at the prospect of being around even more at Malplaquet, but the idea sounded impossible. 'This is not a rainy day – this is a rainy *season*. We're talking *monsoons*. The fees are thousands!'

Unperturbed, Granny went over to her sideboard. 'It's about time you saw this – and you as well, Vicky.' She pulled out a large red hard-backed book.

'Hang on,' said Vicky. 'I've seen that before. Old Smelly had one – is there a picture of the Corinthian Arch near the back?'

Granny was interested to hear the villain had his own copy, but she carried on. 'Let me show you some pictures.' She began to flick her way through the drawings; an old woman and a miserable vicar by an ornate fireplace, the huge Triumphal Arch, another of a bearded old man sat by a small ruined obelisk, and finally a large box floating in a lake below a Cascade. Some little people were pulling it ashore with ropes. 'This is a children's story,' she continued, 'written many years ago. Like most stories, some of it's true.'

'Are you talking about its meaning?' asked Jamie.

'Partly,' replied Granny, 'but I was mainly thinking of an event – and a person. Let me read you the start.' She turned to the first page, and began:

Maria was ten years old. She had dark hair in two pigtails, and brown eyes the colour of marmite but more shiny. She wore spectacles for the time being, though she would not have to wear them always, and her nature was a loving one.

She stopped. Jamie looked at Granny, or rather behind her, at a faded photo on the piano. It showed her as a young girl, a girl with dark hair in two pigtails. Jamie guessed her eyes would have been brown, and more shiny than Marmite.

She opened the inside cover. Across its two pages was a drawing of a landscape garden. In the centre was a large mansion. Throughout the grounds were scattered several buildings and temples, some of which looked similar to ones they knew. The picture was entitled, *The Palace of Malplaquet.*

Jamie could only just find the words to say. 'It's about you?'

Granny gently smiled. 'Not quite. It's a story about someone rather like me – and gardens like Malplaquet. A long time ago. Before the mansion was a school.' She paused, swallowing slightly.

'When it was my home.'

Nigriff was listening respectfully. Jamie and Vicky watched as she gently let her fingers trace their way round the grounds. She stopped by an island in the middle of the larger lake (called the *Upper Sea*).

'Mistress Masham's Repose,' she said wistfully.

'Where you found them?' whispered Vicky. Granny nodded.

'So were *you* the owner that built the model city?' asked Jamie. Another nod. 'And then you sold the place off?'

'I'm sorry to say that you're right.' Granny (Maria) then explained that when still only twenty she had inherited Malplaquet in a poor condition, and had soon spent the limited funds on restoring and then trying to maintain the huge estate. Looking back on it, she had perhaps been *slightly* extravagant – too many overdressed footmen, too many gardeners – but she had been young and inexperienced. Selling it as a school (and investing the money) had become her only option. Fortunately the new Board of Governors had let her live in a cottage behind one of the Lake Pavilions, from where she had kept an eye on her precious little friends.

It had not been easy. The Great Divergence from the city was distressing, as was the Lilliputians consequently forgetting their background. Her only hope had been Pope's prophecy, which she had found in the cellars of the House. Its promise of a future, when the 'Garden Kingdom' would reappear with the Guide's help, had been a comfort in her darkest days.

'So who wrote this book?' asked Vicky.

'One of the first teachers at the school, Mr T.H. White, who taught English, and absolutely loved the place. He wrote children's stories, King Arthur, that sort of thing.'

'Did he know about the people?'

'Never,' replied Granny. 'But I was worried that somebody might hear about them, so I suggested to him a story about a young girl called Maria who found some Lilliputians living at Malplaquet – nobody looks for Alice and Wonderland, do they? We talked over some ideas – how they came to be here, hiding on the island, the model city, things like that. He developed it all and wrote this wonderful book.' She stopped to gather her thoughts. 'It was always going to be a bit of a risk, but I think it worked, or at least it did until now. I've made a huge mistake.' She pulled out a handkerchief to dab at her eyes. 'It's all my fault.'

Nigriff found the right words to say. 'It's not your fault, Madam. You have been a splendid protector for as long as I can remember. You should not chide yourself. I can guarantee that, like Gulliver himself, your illustrious name will feature large in the annals of Lilliput.' He finished with a gracious bow in her direction.

'Over to me now, I suppose,' said Jamie.

'To *us*,' corrected Vicky. 'Team game, remember? Don't forget me helping out in the grounds at weekends.'

'And you need my money,' added Granny, cheering up slowly.

'And would you have a place for an ex-Archivist, sir?'

Jamie just smiled. The Thompson Quad Squad, Mark II.

Let battle commence.

The initial struggle was with Mum and Dad. The request to go to Malplaquet School seemed outrageous, partly because of the very late and sudden decision, but mainly it was the money. Jamie was having to work hard on his parents.

'It's true, Dad, Granny has said she'll pay the fees. And for Charlie as well if he wants to go later on.'

'But why would she do that? And there's no *way* she can afford it – for five years, for both of you?'

'No, honestly, she *can* – she's going to cash in some investments.'

'Seriously?' Dad was shocked. 'I thought she might have a few tucked away somewhere, but I'm staggered if she can raise that much. And why you two?'

'She said we're the nearest thing to a family she's got,' said Jamie. 'She's nobody else to spend it on.'

'Well, I think it's brilliant if it's true,' said Mum. 'Amazingly generous. But I think we'd better talk to her first.'

Once Mr. Thompson had confirmed the financial offer with Granny, he happily accepted the plan. He was particularly excited about a wonderful new 'Visual Education' course that Jamie could study at Malplaquet School, all about buildings and landscapes, which was really useful for budding architects.

Two matters had to be sorted out immediately. First, to contact the Admissions Tutor at Malplaquet to see if there actually was a place available, and then to arrange for some form of Entrance Assessment.

Jamie wondered if he might be taught by Horatius Gratton . . . especially on the tennis courts.

Three days later Mr. Thompson and his elder son, who was looking as smart as he had ever done in his life, walked up the wide and ancient front steps of Malplaquet School. At the top under the imposing portico stood the beaming figure of the Admissions Tutor, exam papers under his arm.

'Morning, Chris,' said Jamie's Dad. 'Thanks for seeing us at short notice.'

'No problem,' he replied, 'always happy to see good boys. In fact, once you get past this little lot, Jamie, you'll have one of the last two places for this September. I saw the other lad yesterday.'

'Is he a local boy?' asked Mr. Thompson.

'No, but he will be. His family's moving to the area; the father's relocating the business, said he's always loved the gardens. What's his name? Something odd beginning with B . . . Biggle? Bundle?'

'Biddle,' said Jamie calmly, not in the least surprised.

The Tutor looked at him. 'That's right – do you know him?'

'Not exactly – but I've heard his name mentioned.'

'Good – nice he's already known in the area. Anyway, come on, let's see you make mincemeat of these papers.' They walked through the main doors.

'Interesting,' thought Jamie. 'Biddle's made his next move already.'

At the end of the afternoon, Jamie was back at the cottage. He was packing. His parents had insisted he spend the rest of the holiday preparing for his new school. Dad was also keen that Granny shouldn't run up a large food bill, bearing in mind future major expenses.

Jamie kept stopping as he found reminders of the last few weeks.

The map of the grounds, used in the 'Golf War' briefing by Thorclan.

A Rubik's Cube.

A National Trust Guidebook, open at a page of an old map, showing the curvy paths of the later gardens.

A copy of *Gulliver's Travels*.

A couple of Scrabble tiles.

And a red plastic dart under a sock. 'Good we found the bow,' he thought.

Granny popped in. 'Don't forget this.' She handed Jamie a large red book. 'You might like to read the story. Look after it, won't you?' Jamie took it off her. 'Oh, another thing. One last trip. We're expected at the Gothic Temple. Vicky's outside in the GT with Thorclan and Nigriff. Yenech should be here as well, but we can't find him.' Jamie briefly wondered if the Listener would be outlining his punishment, but the old lady was smiling, so he felt he shouldn't be worried.

Granny drove the long way round to the Temple, luckily coming across Yenech en route, so they approached it via the avenue of Cypress trees.

Going past the first one, out popped a family of Palladians, both the parents with their three girls, applauding loudly and carrying a banner. The tiny writing said, '*Build a great future with Wesel.*'

To their right was another, held up by Hondall. '*Yenech – clueless no more.*'

The GT's progress down the tree-lined track was slower than ever. Lilliputians appeared all the way along, clapping and cheering, and following the vehicle.

Jamie spotted Troyal, happily sat on a squirrel ('L'-Class), and further on, Sevegar, the Grecian runner.

Vicky was delighted to see Cyrep – and his cousin, Cirep, who was looking none the worse for wear. Her banner said, '*Nothing wet about Hyroc.*'

Granny noticed Hamnob, the Palladian who had planned to start military training. There she was with her aged mother, obviously still very close.

By the time the GT arrived at the Temple, the crowd had swelled to a considerable size. Granny had noticed that different provincials were all mixing together, and was smiling and tearful. The three adults (remember, Jamie was a *Child no More*) and the three Lilliputians approached the old door, to be welcomed by Yeda.

'Good afternoon, sir, and ladies, lovely to see you. Would you like a seat *downstairs*?'

As they entered, the cheering grew even louder. The upper gallery was packed with Lilliputians, madly throwing hats or scarves in the air. More banners were draped over the edge. '*Thorclan is GLOB – again!*' and '*Marry me, Vicky*' (that one had a signature, possibly starting with 'Y'). There was also an enormous red and white one, beyond Lilliputian dimensions, simply saying, '*Happy Holidays!*'

Granny waved at the crowds, to even louder cheering. It didn't last long.

'QUIET!'

The Listener was standing in the centre of the rug. The noise from the gallery rapidly died down. The PRs, Thorclan included, took their places on the usual green band. Jamie felt awkward and stood still, Vicky and Granny by his side.

Vingal composed herself to speak. There was silence throughout the room. 'This is not a normal Assembly, but we should observe the usual manners and conventions. Unseemly behaviour is not acceptable.' She looked around her, and then at Jamie. 'Young man, the last time we met, I was about to present the details of your deserved punishment. You were saved by the interruption of your female friend. Since then, there have been developments.'

Jamie thought this sounded very hopeful.

'Since your arrival, the provinces have suffered a period of unprecedented turbulence, culminating in the intrusion of the heavily odoured camp-dweller. I now understand, however, that all this may not be of *your* making. Furthermore, your recent exploits in saving Yenech, and helping to rescue Cirep and Tuckted, show that we should trust you. The simple fact is that we need *you* to be our Guide.'

There was polite applause from the PRs, and even cheers upstairs from some children, who didn't know any better.

'As a consequence, we would like to formally ask you to take your place beyond the fringe, on the inner circle – the green band.'

Jamie edged forward, uncertain about exactly who to sit next to.

'You do not need to find *one* particular place. Your job will be to represent the interests of *all* the provinces.' He squatted next to the General, several others happily squeezing sideways to make room. Granny and Vicky led the applause.

As the Listener continued her speech, she mentioned the valuable contribution of other smaller people in the recent campaign, and they were duly rewarded. Hyroc was allowed to keep the enormous crossbow, and Wesel was given the honour of being named as Director of Recycling for the provinces.

Lilliputians appeared all the way along, clapping and shouting.

Thorclan was re-awarded his title of GLOB, and had another one added for good measure – Supreme Commander at Battles (SCAB). In his short speech of acceptance, he said that he would have picked that one himself.

Yenech, the brains behind the crossbow assault, was given a small key and an explanation. 'This is a symbol of your award. It represents an open door throughout all the provinces, the *Freedom of Malplaquet.*'

Vicky was thrilled. Granny said he'd got that one a long time ago.

The part played by those two bigger people was also acknowledged, but they refused any honour, saying it was reward enough to continue looking after the inhabitants of Malplaquet. 'Our greatest privilege,' was how Vicky put it, and Granny thought what fine young people there were in society these days.

That left one still to be acknowledged. 'Where is the former Senior Imperial Archivist?' demanded the Listener.

There was a commotion at the back. A few people stood to one side, allowing Nigriff to step forward.

'Approach the rug.' He did so. 'Nigriff, a few days ago you were convicted of most serious charges, and this court stripped you of your position. Since then you have shown remarkable *courage*, first evident when you tried to quell a hostile audience by reciting eighteenth-century poetry. You have also risked your life by tackling humans themselves – even using *their* weaponry. Beyond this, you recently chanced further hostility by discussing with me serious matters of state.'

'So that's what happened,' thought Jamie.

'Good old Nigriff!' whispered Granny.

'I cannot pretend,' continued the Listener, 'that I accept all of your ideas. But they are serious enough to warrant further investigation. As a result, I am asking you to further research that poem, and to make a thorough examination of the Pebble Alcove. Of course, to do that, you will need your title. Unfortunately it has already been given to your deputy. I can only grant you a new one.'

She held a tightly-rolled scroll in front of her. 'Nigriff,

Permanent Grand Archivist, accept this from the people of Malplaquet. It is long overdue.'

To loud cheers Nigriff made his way forwards. He seemed almost overcome, and also embarrassed. When he reached Vingal, he whispered something in her ear. She was visibly shocked, and held up her hand for silence. The applause ceased.

Nigriff looked up nervously. 'I'm awfully sorry, but I can't possibly accept this. All my life I have upheld the highest standards in my professions, as an Archivist and as a Librarian. I'm afraid I cannot possibly, under any circumstances, or for any reason, keep anything that is overdue.'

There was a stunned silence – and then one person's laughter. Nigriff's.

'I do apologise – I thought that it might provoke some merriment. Please do not misunderstand me. Of course I will accept it – this is a great honour.' The whole room joined in with the fun. It was an historic moment – Nigriff's first joke.

Jamie was now standing by Granny. 'Where's he been? Making jokes? It's a bigger change than rowing on the lake. He's become so different this summer.'

'Don't speak too soon,' said Granny. 'He's making his acceptance speech.'

'I must thank my glorious Elysian forbears, people of remarkable intellectual ability, academics of repute, noble and virtuous, famed for their wisdom. . . .'

The three crept out and left them all to it. There was no stopping him now.

That evening Mr. Thompson was driving out of Malplaquet, one of Britain's finest and largest landscaped gardens. He was questioning his son, Jamie, who was returning home after an extended holiday with an elderly family friend.

'You're absolutely sure about starting school here, aren't you?'

'Definitely. I know the place pretty well already.'

'What about making new friends?'

'It's not a *big* problem,' replied his son, remembering his new small friends.

'It won't be what you're used to though, Jamie. All schools are different – they have their own ways of doing things, new words to pick up.'

'That's okay,' said Jamie, as they crossed the humpbacked bridge. 'As you always say right here, Dad, it's like being in another world. I'm really looking forward to it.'

As they drove out through the imposing gates, Jamie smiled happily – as did all the stone faces on the bridge behind them. They were delighted with the events of the summer so far. The Empire had at last begun again, and it looked to be in safe hands.

No matter what might happen next.

The Prophecy

A Child no more, the Man appears,

He comes of Age, the Hope of Years.

Our Fount of Wisdom, whose Way is Delight,

True Source of all Pure Knowledge and Insight,

Our Guide, for whom the Bells do Ring,

Thy Presence much Warmth in Friendship Bring.

Thou makest the Sea-people great Appear,

This Blessed Island shalt have no Fear.

In every Quarter defend our Shores,

Unite our People, grow strong in Wars.

The Capital gained, our Frontiers Sealed,

Temples Restored, the Nation Healed.

Through thee the Great Empire newly Starts,

The Garden Kingdom, true Home of our Hearts.

after Alexander Pope

Don't miss the second story in the Malplaquet trilogy.

The Lost People of Malplaquet

by

Andrew Dalton

The mystery deepens and darkens in this second book, and we learn far more about the strange landscape of Malplaquet, its secret inhabitants, and their possible future.

Biddle takes over a nearby Manor House, strengthens his power locally, and his son John starts at Malplaquet School.
  • How will this affect Jamie and the Lilliputians?
  • Can Nigriff solve the mystery of the Gulliver images in the Pebble Alcove?
  • Will the statues remain as bystanders?
  • What does 'gaining the capital' mean?

And, in the meantime, Charlie begins to uncover some of his brother's secrets. . . .

Will Jamie continue to be the Guide for the tiny people, and with his friends actually bring about the new Empire of Lilliput? Only if, according to Nigriff, he and the Forces of Restoration can prove to be stronger than the Forces of Destruction. . . .